Static

Grosset & Dunlap

GROSSET & DUNLAP
Published by the Penguin Group
Penguin Group (USA) Inc., 375 Hudson Street, New York, New York 10014, U.S.A.
Penguin Group (Canada), 90 Eglinton Avenue East, Suite 700, Toronto, Ontario, Canada M4P 2Y3
(a division of Pearson Penguin Canada Inc.)
Penguin Books Ltd, 80 Strand, London WC2R 0RL, England
Penguin Ireland, 25 St Stephen's Green, Dublin 2, Ireland
(a division of Penguin Books Ltd)
Penguin Group (Australia), 250 Camberwell Road, Camberwell, Victoria 3124, Australia
(a division of Pearson Australia Group Pty Ltd)
Penguin Books India Pvt Ltd, 11 Community Centre, Panchsheel Park, New Delhi - 110 017, India
Penguin Group (NZ), Cnr Airborne and Rosedale Roads, Albany, Auckland 1310, New Zealand
(a division of Pearson New Zealand Ltd)
Penguin Books (South Africa) (Pty) Ltd, 24 Sturdee Avenue, Rosebank, Johannesburg 2196, South Africa

Penguin Books Ltd, Registered Offices:
80 Strand, London WC2R 0RL, England

Library of Congress Control Number: 2005023471

ISBN 0-448-44106-3   10 9 8 7 6 5 4 3 2 1

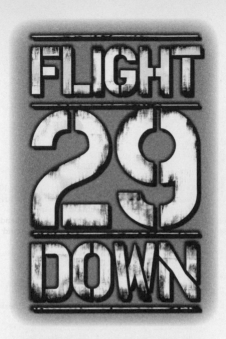

Static

A novelization by
Walter Sorrells
Adapted from the
teleplays by D.J. MacHale

Based on the
TV series created by
D.J. MacHale
Stan Rogow

A Stan Rogow Book · Grosset & Dunlap

There are but five things without which the explorer cannot survive. Water, food, fire, shelter, leadership. And of these the last is most important. For without leadership, the expedition becomes but a mob and the other four will soon disappear. Fear, greed, and anger will then prevail. All will be lost.

—From *The Extensive Perambulations and Adventures of Nathaniel Edmund McHugh, Negro Explorer*, published 1924, Taylor & Taylor, New York

ONE

Nathan

Okay, okay, okay ... so, my name's Nathan. I hope this video isn't too wobbly or whatever. As you can see, I'm sitting in the back of this little propeller airplane and it's kind of shaking around, so ... Anyway, don't worry about the lightning and stuff. I asked the pilot about it and he was like, "Kid, we have four engines. What could go wrong?" So I'm cool with that.

Whoa! Sorry. Man, that was kind of a big one.

Hey! Guys! Do you have to be so loud? I'm trying to record something here!

Sorry. Anyway. So here's the 411. There're ten of us on this plane. We're all students at the Hartwell School outside Los Angeles. We're flying to this little island in the South Pacific called Palau. We're going on an eco-camping trip. I am so stoked. We've been busting our butts for, like, a year now doing car washes and bake sales and stuff to raise money for the trip. And now it's finally on.

Yeah! It's totally on!

So, Palau. Supposedly this island Palau has these amazing jungles and beaches and there are all these breeds of animals and plants that you can only find—

Whoa! Man, did you see that stuff flying around the cabin behind me? We must have hit an air pocket or something. Seriously. Did you see it? I don't know if the camera picked it up or not. Here, I'll pan around the cabin. See that girl? That's my girlfriend, Taylor Hagan—well, my ex-girlfriend. Anyway, when we hit the air pocket her mp3 player went flying, like, three feet in the air.

Whoa!

Okay. You know what? Dude, I'm sitting down. Hey, I'm not scared. Come on. But seriously, if—

Captain Robert Russell, the pilot of the four-engined DeHavilland Heron, wore a Hawaiian shirt with pineapples on it. That morning pineapples had seemed like the perfect choice. Tropical and carefree. He was into Hawaiian shirts. Every shirt had its own message, its own vibe. You had to have the right shirt or you wouldn't be in the zone. And flying planes was all about being in the zone.

Right now was not feeling like a real pineapple moment. He should have worn the shirt with tigers on it.

He'd spent the last forty-five minutes vectoring around this storm, trying to find a way through. Where had the storm come from? It hadn't been on any of the forecasts! So far, he hadn't found any breaks in the squall. There'd been sixty, seventy-knot headwinds, crazy downdrafts, sudden side winds. Basically the plane was getting beaten to death.

BAM! A huge bolt of lightning shot through the sky, illuminating the massive black thunderheads all around the plane.

He tapped the compass. Something about it didn't seem right. The plane was forty-six years old—the exact same age as Captain Russell. Gauges were always going out. Situation normal. But not the compass. Nothing ever went wrong with a compass.

A sudden crosswind rolled the plane sideways. Captain Russell jerked the yoke, hit the rudder, wiped sweat off his brow. He was having trouble maintaining his heading in these crosswinds.

He looked over his shoulder. The kids back in the cabin seemed oblivious to the storm. One boy was standing up making a video of himself and another was wandering up and down the aisle harassing the other kids.

Captain Russell hadn't always been flying rattletrap old planes like this. Twenty years ago he'd been a captain in the air force, flying KC-130 refueling planes—one of the most demanding flying jobs you could have in the military. But he had never fit in with the military way of doing things, though, and so the air force had eventually given him the old heave-ho. (The day he'd shown up for duty wearing a Hawaiian shirt under his flight suit had pretty much sealed the deal.)

After he left the military, he'd flown for a big airline for a couple of years. But once again, his personality had rubbed all his bosses the wrong way. "You're a great pilot, Bob," they'd all say, "but here's the thing . . ." And then they'd tell him to clear out his locker. Getting along with people was never his strong suit. Since then it had been a series of third-rate charter jobs, flying birds that got sketchier and older by the day.

And now here he was, stuck with a bunch of *kids*. Why couldn't some of the adult chaperones have flown on this plane? They had all stampeded onto the other plane, leaving him with the responsibility for ten loudmouth, won't-sit-down, won't-do-what-you-tell-them kids. *Thank you very much, guys. Thank you so very, very much. This is just what I needed.*

Should have called in sick, let Ramirez or Coco fly this bunch of spoiled brats. Right about now he'd have been sitting on his deck watching the sun go down and sipping on a—

BAM!

That one sounded way too close!

The plane bucked.

Captain Russell looked over his shoulder. "Hey! Buckle in! Now!"

He kicked the rudder again, fighting the crosswind. The plane was doing something weird, yawing like crazy. Even at full rudder he was losing his heading. It felt like his two right engines had gone out on him. Which obviously was impossible.

He looked out the window at the right wing. Where there had been engines, now there was nothing but a sheet of flame.

"Kids! Now!" he screamed. "How many times do I have to tell you?"

Eric McGorrill stumbled down the aisle of the crappy old plane with his water bottle in his hand, getting ready. He was gonna totally nail these geeks. Every gag, you had to bait the hook. His old man had told him that. His dad, the famous comedy writer. The only useful advice his old man had ever given him. Set up the gag, son, always set up the gag.

So he made a big face, like he felt all sick. "Oh, man," he said loudly. "I don't feel so great!"

"Hey, guys, do you have to be so loud?" Nathan McHugh yelled at him. "I'm trying to record something." Nathan. Mr. Perfect. At least that's what he thought he was. A Mr. Perfect wannabe.

Eric knew that perfection was out. No way he'd ever be perfect. So he was working on funny. Besides, only dorks wanted to be perfect. Perfection was so boring. Funny was cool. Funny also got you out of work, out of jams, out of all kinds of stuff. While people were laughing, they didn't pay attention to the fact that you were playing them like cheap violins.

"I . . . I think I'm losing it!" Eric yelled. Then he made a real good ralphing noise and squirted water in Taylor's lap. "Airsick!"

"Ahhhhh! Gross! Gross!" Taylor yelled. She had been looking through *InStyle* magazine. Now she started whaling on him with the magazine. It was, like, an inch thick. Man, it was like getting hit with a plank! Taylor—totally hot Taylor—was beating his butt. This wasn't going according to plan.

He retreated a few steps, laughing loudly, and considered pretending to puke on Lex, the little kid. Nah, boring. Lex was Daley's younger brother—this little geek, nine or ten years old. He'd probably start talking about the chemical composition of water or something.

Behind Eric, Melissa Wu stood up with her water bottle, made a pathetic puking noise and tried to squirt it on Taylor, too. Melissa was something Asian. Chinese? Japanese? Korean? Eric could never keep it straight. Anyway, how lame, trying to steal his joke! What was up with that?

Taylor grabbed the water bottle from Melissa, heaved it down the aisle. It hit Eric in the head.

"Grow *up!*" Taylor yelled.

Melissa smiled hesitantly, then looked at Eric like she was seeking approval. Eric gave her his sleepy-eyed face. Like, *Yeah, whatever.* Melissa sat back down looking like somebody all embarrassed and hurt. What a loser. Eric smirked.

Outside the little plane, thunder and lightning were banging away. The wind was dogging the plane so hard that it was throwing him all over the aisle. It was pretty cool, actually. Not quite as good as a roller coaster. But close. Somewhere between a dirt bike and a—

BAM!

Eric laughed. That was some serious lightning! Up in the front of the plane, the pilot in the Hawaiian shirt was raving about something. Eric tuned him out, sucked some water into his mouth, made another gagging noise, and leaned over toward Daley Marin. Yeah, that would be good. Nail the class president.

Only, Daley—Little Miss Hypercompetitive—was too quick for him. She squirted him in the face.

"Good one!" Eric said. You always got points for giving other people credit—even if you didn't really mean it.

Next thing he knew, everybody was getting into it— squirting water and spitting and laughing. Eric stepped back to watch the mayhem he'd created.

BAM!

The plane dropped, and for an extremely long moment Eric felt like he was floating weightlessly in midair. Which meant the whole plane was free-falling!

BAM! A second explosion.

Eric blinked. Okay, that was a lot scarier than riding a dirt bike.

"Buckle in! *Now!*" the pilot yelled at them again.

Eric stood frozen for a second, then he looked out the

window. It looked like there were flames coming out of the engines. Which was not possible. That kind of stuff didn't happen in real life.

Still, he thought. *Maybe I'd better.*

As he headed toward his seat, the plane did something really weird and creepy. *Was that my imagination?* he thought. *Or did this crappy old plane just go upside down for a second?*

He started moving toward Taylor. She looked terrified. Beautiful! Totally hot chicks always had their guard up. You had to wait for that perfect moment. Like a time of crisis.

Eric started moving toward Taylor. What was he going to say? You always had to have an opening line. *What about: I'm here for you? Was that too uncool?*

The plane seemed to tip sideways, then Eric felt like he was on a slide, back in the playground days. Only it wasn't him that was sliding. It was the whole plane.

Someone started to scream.

TWO

Nathan looked out the window. The main thing he saw was fire. Flames and smoke trailed from both of the engines on the right wing.

Okay, that would pretty much be the official signal to sit down and put on his seatbelt.

Before he sat down, he had to know if they had any power at all. He hopped up, looked out the other window. The other two engines were still working. That was good. The plane was suddenly rocked by a huge buffet of wind. Things went flying around the cabin. An mp3 player, a single shoe, a soda can. For a moment they seemed to levitate. Then they slammed back down.

He jumped back into his seat next to Melissa Wu, his best friend. She was staring straight in front of her, eyes wide open. Her lips were moving, but he couldn't hear what she was saying.

"It's gonna be okay, Mel!" he said. Probably more to convince himself than to convince her.

Nathan's great-great-grandfather had been this famous explorer a long time ago. He had written about his adventures in a book that Nathan had read so many times, he'd about memorized it. Nathan's life was so normal and predictable that every time he'd crack open the book, he felt a slight tinge of envy for the many hardships of his great-great-grandfather's life. Sitting around in his nice house in Brentwood, it had seemed really cool when his great-great-grandfather had written, *I have been in perhaps five or six predicaments so severe that I felt quite certain I would not live to see another sunrise.*

But now that Nathan was looking out the window at the two flaming engines as they flew somewhere over the endless ocean, he wished that he was home in Brentwood, lying on his bed with his dog Mickey and his annoying little sister and his mom out in the hallway bugging him about cleaning his room. He was so frightened that his pulse was hammering in his ears and his legs and arms felt limp.

Two seats in front of Nathan, an underclassman named Jory was screaming unrelentingly.

The door to the pilot's cabin kept banging open and shut, open and shut, open and shut. The pilot was hunched over his controls. Suddenly he whipped around and barked, "Somebody shut that girl up!" His face and balding forehead were streaming with sweat—though the plane felt kind of chilly to Nathan.

The pilot turned back to his controls.

At first I was seized by a terrible, near-petrifying fear, Nathan's great-great-grandfather had written. *But then in each time of ultimate distress a sudden calm descended upon my brain and I found myself able to think with the utmost clarity. While other men's courage failed, I leapt into action unencumbered by concern for anything save what the moment required. And so, by the curious gift of my God-given constitution, I prevailed.*

Sudden calm? When would that sudden calm come? All Nathan could think of was that he wanted to scream like that girl Jory up in the front of the cabin.

What were they gonna do? What were they gonna do?

Out the window the streak of flame behind the engines had gotten longer, brighter.

Captain Russell was dumping altitude as fast as he could. Under perfect circumstances, the plane could hold altitude on two engines. These were not perfect circumstances. Sudden tailwinds were dropping his airspeed to nothing. Headwinds were kicking his nose up. Every time he tried to steady his altitude, the plane would threaten to stall. The altimeter was reading 4,200 feet. 4,100. 4,000.

Why hadn't he worn his lucky shirt? And where was the life raft? If they hit water absolutely perfectly, the plane would float for maybe a minute. Which *might* be enough time to dig through all the mountain of camping junk these kids were carrying and get to the raft. And if they hit the water wrong, busted up the airframe? The DeHavilland would take on water and sink like a lead brick.

Captain Russell wiped his face again. The sweat was pouring in his eyes, making it hard to see. In front of him there was nothing but blackness.

3,400. 3,300.

He had to face facts here. They were gonna ditch. And into what kind of seas? A big storm like this could kick up thirty- and forty-foot swells out here in the Pacific. If they landed in that kind of water, it was all over.

He turned and looked behind him. "Hey! You!" he yelled to a kid wearing a dorky-looking straw hat.

"Me?" The kid pointed to his chest. His face was white as a ghost.

"You! Go to the back of the plane. There's a life raft in the emergency—" A tailwind slammed them and the DeHavilland stalled. Captain Russell turned to the controls, kicked the yoke forward. The DeHavilland lost three hundred feet before he got it under control again.

He looked over his shoulder again. "There's a life raft in the emergency closet in the back of the plane. Go get it out!"

"Yeah, right," the kid said, tightening his seatbelt and then closing his eyes. "I'm not going anywhere."

Another gust of wind, this time from the left wing. The whole plane rolled ninety degrees. The ancient airframe moaned under the pressure.

"I don't have time for this!" Captain Russell yelled. "Get the—" But the kid in the hat had his eyes squeezed shut. The blond girl next to him didn't look any better. "You!" he yelled to a springy-haired kid. "Nathan! Isn't that your name?"

The kid blinked, stared at him.

"Somebody get back there and get the life raft out!"

"Are we gonna crash?" the kid yelled.

Captain Russell scowled and turned back to the controls. 2,800 feet. The winds had lessened for a moment. Maybe they'd break out of the storm. Maybe he could hold this altitude for a little while. And then what? Wait for the fire to hit the gas tanks and blow the wing off? It wasn't a question of whether they ditched or not. It was only a question of when.

And where.

The life raft? Nathan felt like he was hyperventilating. *The life raft.* If the captain wanted him to get the life raft out, then that meant they were about to crash. In the ocean.

Nathan had seen TV shows about people stranded in weather like this. Things didn't usually turn out that great. Even if you made it into the water in one piece, even if you got into the life rafts—sixty-mile-an-hour winds would catch you at the top of a thirty-foot wall of water and flip your raft like a bottle cap.

A sudden calm descended upon me.

Where was it? Where was the sudden calm?

He staggered to his feet. He could feel his teeth chattering. He headed toward the rear of the plane.

Daley Marin was already there, her back to him. She was a thin, athletic girl with long, wavy reddish-blond hair. There was a panel on the back wall of the plane that said "EMERGENCY." Daley was fumbling with the latch to open it.

She looked over her shoulder. Her face was pale, but her jaw was firm and her eyes flashed. "Help me, Nathan," she said.

The plane suddenly dropped. Gear slid across the floor—backpacks, a canteen, some plastic boxes. Earlier they been secured to the bulkhead, but evidently the bungee cords had given way. The camping equipment was all piling up against the door.

"Now, Nathan!" Daley shouted. "Get all this gear clear so I can open the door."

Nathan felt frozen. He stared at all the stuff piled up against the door. Jory was still screaming in the front of the plane. "We're gonna die!" she shouted. "I don't want to die!" The screaming was really, really, really making it hard to concentrate.

"What are you *doing*?" Daley shouted. "Move the stuff!"

Nathan finally shook his head and started grabbing backpacks, heaving them over his shoulders. It was kind of a relief to be doing something instead of sitting there waiting for the wing to fall off.

Daley finally got the door open. Inside was an orange plastic life raft rolled up into a cylinder about the size of the turkey smoker Nathan's dad had bought for Thanksgiving last year.

"Stop daydreaming and help me!" Daley yelled.

There was a strap around the life raft with a metal clasp attached to it. Nathan grabbed the handle and yanked. "Wait," Daley said. "Not yet! I'm not ready!"

But it was too late. The clasp came free and the raft immediately started falling off its mount on the bulkhead. Daley tried to grab it, but the weight of the raft was too much for her. They fell backward into a heap, smashing against the rearmost seat in the plane.

"Everybody sit down and assume crash positions!" someone yelled.

Daley seemed frozen. She was staring at something. "Look what you did," she said accusingly.

"Get back in your seats!" It was Captain Russell. "Buckle up!"

"Wha—?" Nathan said. His tongue seemed glued to the roof of his mouth.

Daley pointed wordlessly.

As they'd fallen, the raft had slammed into the metal seat frame. Apparently there had been a sharp piece of metal sticking out of the frame, because there was now a

six-inch-long gash in the orange rubber skin of the life
raft.

"Why didn't you catch it?" Nathan said.

"It's your fault! I wasn't ready!" Daley said.

Nathan had been distracted from his fear for a moment.
But now his distraction was gone. He knew what the maps of
this part of the world looked like. Blue. Nothing but blue—
with only a few tiny specks of green, like pepper scattered
across the map. The odds of hitting land out here were
zilch.

And without the life raft? They were dead.

"In your seats!" The whole plane had begun to vibrate
now. Something was bad—this wasn't just the weather.
Something was going very wrong with the plane.

Nathan tried to stand, but his legs didn't want to support
him. He began to crawl up the aisle.

Captain Russell felt the shuddering in his feet first.
Something had gone wrong with the rudder and he was
getting feedback through the pedals like someone was
tapping on the soles of his shoes. Then the plane itself
began shaking.

1,800 feet. 1,700.

He looked back, saw the two kids had gotten the life
raft free. Alright, well, that was something. If he could
hold the plane together when they ditched, maybe they'd
have a ghost of a chance. He hollered at the kids to sit
down.

He looked back out the windscreen. At some point they
had to break out of the cloud cover. Then he'd see how bad
it was going to be.

700. 650. 625.

Come on! Come on, stupid plane! The whole plane was shuddering rhythmically now, and it had gotten nearly impossible to keep his heading. He was at full right/left rudder. But the plane wasn't responding.

Suddenly the gray-black outside the windscreen lightened. It turned light gray, then flickered, flickered, flickered—and they were free!

575 feet.

The black clouds scudded by above them like a ceiling of hammered lead.

He could see the ocean now. An unbroken stretch of it, a dark hellish green flecked with windblown spume. How high were the waves? It was hard to tell from up here. Big. That was the bottom line. Anything over ten feet would rip the plane up for sure.

550. 525.

Over his shoulder the right engines were burning brightly. The fire would be softening up the structural members. How soon before they gave out and the wing came off?

Suddenly, out of the corner of his eye, he saw something. For a moment, he was sure . . .

He whirled around. To his left was a wall of clouds.

Wait! No! A flash of green.

Surely not. He was hallucinating. But there it was again. Yes! An island! Then it was gone again.

How far away? Six miles? Seven?

He'd have to bank, bring the DeHavilland around, head into the wind and hope they could make it. They were holding at 500 feet. Airspeed, 105 knots. They'd lose altitude on the bank. Six miles? He didn't see any way they'd make it. But maybe they could swim it.

He raised the right wing a little, slid into a slow bank.

The plane was fighting him the whole time, the two left engines trying to propel him in the other direction. Would they even be able to turn enough to get him all the way around?

The island had disappeared in the cloud again. Wait, there it was, at eight o'clock. Could he get the plane around? Slowly, slowly the plane began turning. The island was at nine o'clock now.

Ten o'clock. Airspeed 95 knots. Just about stall speed. Altitude 325. The waves seemed incredibly close now. They passed over a reef. Huge rollers crashed and hammered at the coral. Fifteen-footers, easy. They'd snap the plane in half like a cheap cigar.

Still, the ancient DeHavilland was coming around, coming around. The island was at eleven o'clock now. Eleven thirty. Almost there. The island was in full view now, a dark forbidding mass of green jungle and sharp volcanic mountains. No place to land.

Airspeed was holding at 95. Russell was holding his breath. Literally. It felt like even if he shifted in his seat, it might stall them out. No margin for error. One stall would put them in the water. But if he dropped too fast trying to pick up speed—well, that would put them in the waves, too.

Okay, the island was at twelve o'clock now: dead ahead. Altitude 250 and dropping. The rudder flapped uselessly behind him. How far was the island? Two miles? Three? Could he keep this crate aloft for another two minutes?

He doubted it.

Captain Russell turned and yelled back at the kids, "Hold on! We're going in!"

Out the window all Nathan could see was water. Nasty black waves, their peaks foaming and spitting in the wind. They didn't have a chance.

Jory Twist continued to howl about how they were all going to die.

Mel was hunched over in the seat next to Nathan. Her legs were shaking.

Outside, the waves were getting closer and closer. How soon before one of them reached up and grabbed the plane and yanked it down into the water?

For a moment Nathan had a brief flash: *What were Mom and Dad doing right now?* Probably sitting around the breakfast table. Dad was probably reading *The Wall Street Journal* and his mom was reading *Opera News* and his little sister Emmy was probably reading some book about astronomy, her latest obsession. He'd said something mean to her about it right before he'd left, called her a "star nut" or something. Would that be the last thing she'd remember about him?

He looked out the window at the waves. The life raft was shot. There had been life preservers in the back, but he hadn't thought to put one on. His great-great-grandfather would never have neglected something that obvious. Not Mr. Unencumbered-by-Concern-Save-for-What-the-Moment-Demanded. The moment demanded a freakin' life preserver. And here he was holding on to his—

The plane shuddered and there was a huge bang, followed by the shock of impact. Nathan's head snapped forward, banging into the seat back in front of him.

A huge spray of water hit the windows. The plane seemed to be airborne again for a moment.

So this is it, Nathan thought. *My big adventure. Oh, well.*

Then he had a sensation in the pit of his stomach, like he was falling out of a tree.

The plane hit again, this time slamming even harder into the waves. There were noises of tearing metal as the plane came to a halt—almost as though they'd run into a brick wall. For a moment nothing moved.

With the life raft punctured, they were pretty much goners. He knew he should do something. But what?

He sat frozen and waited for the plane to sink.

THREE

Silence.

Weird. Why weren't they sinking?

Daley looked out the window. Her eyes widened. She had expected to see them floating in the middle of the water. But they weren't. She couldn't see much. But that wasn't water outside: It was sand.

"You can let go of my knee, Daley," Lex said.

Lex was Daley's little brother. She couldn't be looking all nervous and weak in front of her little brother. Daley jerked her hand away from his knee. "I thought that was the armrest."

Lex looked at her impishly. "Uh-huh."

"Seriously. I was just making sure you're okay."

"Which is it?" Lex said. "Were you making sure I was okay . . . or did you think my knee was the armrest?"

She ignored him, standing quickly and looking around the cabin. "Everybody okay?"

Nathan stood up, too, brushed past Daley and opened

the curtain to the pilot's cabin. Daley followed. The pilot would be able to tell them what was going on.

She looked over Nathan's shoulder into the pilot's cabin. The pilot was a middle-aged guy in a Hawaiian shirt with pineapples on it. Somehow the pineapples didn't exactly inspire confidence.

"Mayday, Mayday," the pilot was saying into the radio. "Two-niner Delta William November. We are down. Coordinates unknown."

Coordinates unknown? That didn't sound good.

"Mayday. Two-niner Delta William November. Bound for Karor Airai out of Guam International. We are down. Mayday, Mayday."

Daley looked around the cabin. A thin trail of smoke wafted through the air, and luggage had spilled all over.

"Are we dead?" Taylor said.

Eric reached over and pinched her.

"Ow!" Taylor squealed.

"Guess not," Eric said.

Taylor slugged him.

The kids were standing up slowly, everybody looking a little shell-shocked. Daley counted heads, pointed at each of the campers in turn, checking to make certain that everyone was okay. Taylor Hagan, Eric McGorrill, Nathan McHugh, Lex—check. Abby Fujimoto, Jory Twist (who had finally stopped screaming, thank God!), Ian Milbauer, Melissa Wu—check. And finally rising from his seat in the back, the mystery guy, Cody Jackson—check. All of the kids looked fine—not even a bloody nose. She tried to look out the window to see the airport where they'd landed, but strangely all she could see were trees and sand. Maybe this was some kind of emergency airstrip.

"Excuse me," Daley said to the pilot. "Are we on Palau?"

The bald, sweating pilot wiped his face. His hands were trembling slightly. He looked up irritably from his radio. "Slight change of plans, sweetheart."

"So where are we?"

The pilot made a sound like he was laughing. But he didn't look like he thought anything was funny. "You tell me." He looked past Nathan and Daley, the radio microphone still in his hand. "Anybody hurt?"

"Go ahead, sir," Nathan said. "You keep working the radio. I'll get things organized back here."

"Whatever," the pilot mumbled. Then he turned a knob on the radio and started talking again.

"Anybody hurt?" Nathan called.

Daley smiled. "All taken care of, Nathan. Everybody's fine. I checked."

"We're gonna be late, Nathan!" Melissa said, her eyes wide. Melissa was a very nice girl, but a little on the nervous side. "We were supposed to meet the rest of the class. And the adults—they're all in the other plane!"

"Gee whiz, don't wanna be late!" Eric said. "That would be a disaster." Eric's eyes widened and he made an exaggerated face of surprise. "Oops! Too late. Already had one."

"Where are we?" Daley said.

"Somewhere," Nathan said. Nathan had been acting all weird since he'd lost the election earlier in the week. They had run against each other for president of the student body and Nathan had lost. It wasn't exactly that he was a sore loser—but every time she'd tried to talk to him since then he'd gotten this look in his eyes like she'd stolen something from him.

Daley shouldered past Nathan, walked up to the pilot's cabin, and stuck her head in again. "Call the other plane. Or the airport on Palau. Or the navy. Or—"

"Yeah, terrific!" The pilot looked up at her and gave her a broad smile. "Oh, hey, I got an idea."

"What's that?" Daley said.

"Maybe I can just tune in to the Yankees game while I'm at it."

Great. The pilot was a comedian. "Not funny."

"You want funny?" The pilot swiveled around, started punching buttons on his radio console. "Listen."

Kksssssssshh! It was pure static.

"Laughing yet?" the pilot said as he turned a switch.

Kshhaaaaahahh.

"Funny enough? Hm? Yeah?"

Ksssssssss. Krraaaaaaaaaaa. Ppppppppp. Rrrrrrrrrrr.

"In case you're wondering," the pilot said, "that's what we call static. That means this radio is about as useless as this plane." He kept turning knobs.

Mmmmmmmm. Kkkkksssssshhhhhh. Ahhhhhhhhhnnnnnn.

"Okay, okay, I get it," Daley snapped. "I just have a simple question. Where. Are. We."

Nathan stepped over to the hatch, twisted the handle, and pushed it open. He had to squint from the sunshine. Daley looked out over his shoulder. The sun shone brightly from the middle of a pure blue sky. Nothing remained of the storm that had knocked their plane out of the sky—nothing but a heavy dark line on the horizon. To the right was a long line of palm trees. In front of them, stretching out for what looked like miles, was the most beautiful white sand beach she had ever seen. To the left was the blue, endless sea.

There was not a human being in sight.

Alone in paradise.

"Here," Nathan said, turning to her. "We're here."

FOUR

Nathan stood in the open hatch of the aircraft for a moment, looking out at the amazing empty beach. Behind him Eric nudged Daley aside and peered out, too.

"Look at that water!" Eric said. "I'm going in!" He clambered down the steps and out into the sand, started peeling off his shirt. Nathan couldn't believe it. This kid was acting like this was ... well ... a day at the beach.

"Hey, Eric," Nathan said. "Reality check. We just nearly bought it."

"Nearly." Eric gave him an amused look. "That's the key word. Is anybody hurt? No."

Melissa stuck her head out the hatch, blinking in the sunlight. "But Eric ... we crashed."

"No duh. But think about it. This trip's done. As soon as they find us, our parents will freak out, and then we'll be on the next plane home. So much for our big vacation."

Melissa looked at him, wide-eyed.

"Come on!" Eric said. He took off his little straw hat, sailed it onto the sand. "I say we have fun while we still have the chance."

Taylor followed Eric onto the sand, looking up at the blue sky, then running her hands through her long blond hair. "Really," she said. "I mean, we're not gonna be here long, right?"

Nathan and Melissa exchanged glances. Melissa's face was still pale. Eric and Taylor just didn't seem to get how serious this was. Nathan looked around, feeling a little numb. This was really not good. Yes, they were still alive. But what now? The way the pilot was talking, they had no way of contacting anybody to tell them where they were. They had precious little food and water. Despite the heat of the sun, Nathan felt a chill run through his body.

Like Eric, Taylor pulled off her outer clothes. She was wearing a bathing suit underneath—already prepared for the beach. Kids started filtering off the plane, looking around with a mix of nervousness and excitement. Everybody watched in shock as Eric and Taylor ran into the waves and started splashing around.

"Just another day at the beach," Jackson said. Without saying another word, he started walking off toward the line of trees.

Nathan

I totally thought I was going to win when I ran for student-council president. Being modest, I'm probably the most popular guy at Hartwell. I don't mean like jerky-jock-popular. I like people. Kids from any background, kids with different interests, whatever. I think I'm a natural leader. So how come so many people voted for Daley?

I mean, sure, she's totally competent. But she's an ego case. If an idea's not hers, it's not a good idea. Man, that gets old quick.

Anyway, I've always been the guy everybody liked. I was student-council president in middle school. I was secretary treasurer of the student body last year. It just seemed natural that I'd be president. I gotta admit, losing kind of took the wind out of my sails.

And then my girlfriend, Taylor, she dumped me like the minute the election results were announced. Talk about humiliating.

It kind of makes you question what you amount to. Maybe being on this island will give me a chance to prove who's the real leader. I mean . . . Daley? Come on! You want somebody to count all the money you raised at the bake sale, she's your girl.

But look at this place. This is the real deal. This ain't a bake sale, boys and girls.

So, yeah. It's time for Nathan McHugh to step up.

"You think Taylor's right?" Melissa said. "You think we're not going to be here long?"

"Hmmm," Nathan said.

"And for that matter—I mean, how long is *long*?" Melissa said.

"Well, *Twenty-Nine Down*'s not going anywhere, that's for sure."

"Twenty-Nine what?" Melissa said.

Nathan pointed at the plane. The DeHavilland had plowed up a long swath of sand when it crashed. "See the numbers on the tail?"

The identifying numbers on the right side of the tail were smudged with soot. But they were still readable: 29 DWN. The soot must have come from the burning engines. Both of the right engines were burned black, their propellers gone. Wisps of smoke still trailed from the wing, and Nathan could smell the burning fuel.

"We're lucky we even made it," Nathan said. "Another five, ten minutes, I bet that wing would have burned right off."

Melissa put her head on her knees. "God, Nathan, we almost died, didn't we?"

Nathan sighed. "It's not over yet, you know. Until we're off this island? We're still in some serious trouble."

"You're scaring me a little," Melissa said.

"I know. But being scared doesn't do us any good," Nathan said. "We need to start figuring out how to survive here. Maybe I should—"

Before he could get his thought out, Daley's little brother, Lex, came up behind them and pulled on Nathan's shirt. He was probably a good kid, but he could be a little annoying. It was obvious to Nathan that somebody needed to look around and see if there was anybody on the island who could help. A little exploration—yeah, that's what he needed to do. He'd grab the camera, get the lay of the land, maybe do an entry in his video diary.

"You know what I think," Lex said. "I—"

"Hold that thought. I'm gonna look around," Nathan said.

Over near the tree line, Nathan could see Jackson looking at him. Jackson—the new kid. He was a scholarship student at Hartwell, the only one of the kids on the plane that Nathan hadn't known for years and years. There was something about Jackson that made Nathan nervous. He had a little of that Slim Shady vibe. There was a rumor going around school that he'd been in juvenile hall or something. Everybody was like, oh, yeah, that Jackson guy used to be in a gang, he used to live over in some crappy neighborhood down in Long Beach or Venice or somewhere, he used to do this, that, and the other. Only nobody really knew.

For a minute Nathan thought about going over to see if Jackson wanted to come explore with him.

Jackson met Nathan's eyes. It was almost like he was challenging Nathan somehow. Then Jackson slipped on his headphones, pulled up the hood on his sweat jacket, and closed his eyes like he'd forgotten Nathan was even there.

Weird. What was up with that guy?

Nathan scanned the area, looked for someplace that would offer a view of the island. A few hundred feet down the beach was a tall dune. That ought to work. He trotted down the beach, imagining what he might see. Maybe there'd be a town or something. He'd been doing a lot of reading about Pacific islands over the past year. There were a lot of cool islands out here. Fiji, Tahiti, Vanuatu, all kinds of crazy places. This island had "tourist paradise" written all over it. Maybe there'd be a hotel or resort or even some little village visible in the distance.

Then he'd be able to come back and tell everybody what he'd found. He'd be the guy who saved them. Very cool.

The dune was bigger than it looked from a distance, dotted with scraggly little vines and plants. He grabbed a vine, started climbing up the dune. It was hard going, the sand slipping out from under his shoes. He fell once, looked over to make sure nobody had seen him. Eric and

Taylor were still goofing around in the surf. Most of the kids were standing around. Except Daley and her little brother—who were busy unpacking camping junk from the plane.

From this distance the plane seemed tiny and fragile, like a spindly little bug. The huge blue swath of ocean dominated everything. It looked like at any moment the ocean could just reach out and sweep everything away. Not that there was much danger of that. The DeHavilland was right up at the edge of the beach. Even with its engines out of commission, the little plane was their lifeline, their connection to civilization. He turned away and headed on up the sandy slope.

He was out of breath by the time he crested the dune. He stared out across the island. His heart sank.

There wasn't a resort or hotel or sign or road or even a plume of smoke to show that some Polynesian islanders were out there roasting a chicken or something. Rising up a few miles away was a steep, forbidding mountain. And between Nathan and the mountain—jungle.

Miles of green, impenetrable jungle.

He turned and looked back at the plane. It looked even more fragile and spindly than it had before.

"This is not good," Nathan said.

Daley was very nervous, very frightened. Yes, they were alive. But what now? Nobody knew where they were. They could be here for a very long time. Daley was the kind of person who dealt with fear by getting busy. There was a lot to do here. Things needed to be organized. Food needed to be inventoried, supplies and water located, tents and sleeping bags unpacked. And what was everybody doing? Goofing around like this was a normal vacation.

Taylor was down in the water showing off her perfect

body; Eric was running after her with his tongue hanging out; Jackson was listening to rap music; Melissa was walking around asking everybody the same questions that nobody had answers for. And Captain Pineapple, the pilot, was making no effort to do anything. He was an adult! He was supposed to be in charge!

At least Lex could be counted on to do what he was told.

"Hey, Daley, I was thinking . . ." Lex said.

Daley put a baseball cap on his head. It had the logo of the Hartwell School on the crown. "Wear this," Daley said. "If you get heatstroke, Mom will kill me."

Eric and Taylor had finally come out of the water and were standing by the airplane watching her work with bemused expressions on their faces.

Daley clapped her hands, started pulling more Hartwell hats out of a box. "Guys! Guys! Hey, attention, everybody. Keep your heads covered or you'll fry."

She tried to hand Taylor a hat, but Taylor held up her palm and made a face of horror. "Omigod, no! I want highlights."

Abby, Jory, and Ian came over and put on their hats. Daley looked around, saw Jackson watching her from the tree line where he was sitting with his back against a palm tree. She held out a hat toward him. He just closed his eyes, adjusted the hood of his ghetto-looking sweat jacket and leaned back against the tree.

Daley narrowed her eyes. He was going to be a problem. If they got stuck here for long, leadership was going to be crucial. And Jackson? She suspected he was one of those kinds of people who just loved undermining other people's authority.

Daley looked around to see who else she could give a hat to. Nathan had wandered off down the beach and was struggling up a dune a few hundred yards away. Typical Nathan. Messing around while real work needed to be done. She watched him stand on top of the hill, staring out at the jungle. He looked a little dejected. He was probably still sulking about the election. How did he expect people to take him seriously? Oh, he meant well. But when it came to getting things done, he was pretty ineffective. No wonder he'd lost the election.

After a minute, he turned to come back down the hill. As he did, he tripped on some kind of vine, went head over heels, falling all the way down to the bottom of the sand dune.

Daley tried not to smile. She reprimanded herself: Nathan was a perfectly nice boy. No point enjoying his misery. *Back to work, Daley. No goofing around.*

As she started organizing the boxes again, she looked around for Lex. He had walked away from the plane and was staring fixedly out at the ocean.

"Daley," Lex said, "I really think—"

"Lex!" Daley said. "What are you doing? I need you over here."

"Yeah, but Daley, I really think—"

"Think later, Lex. Right now it's time to work."

Lex walked slowly toward her, dragging a small piece of driftwood behind him.

Suddenly Captain Pineapple came out of the plane carrying a wrench and the guts of a radio with some wires hanging out of it. His nails had dirt under them.

"Kids!" he yelled. "Children! Yo! Huddle up for a minute."

Well. It was about time the guy finally took charge.

Daley walked over to the shade of a palm tree where the pilot was standing.

"Uh, kids, my name is Captain Russell. Just wanted to

give you a heads-up on where we're at."

"We're at the beach, bro!" Eric said.

Captain Russell ignored him. "Look, I ain't no camp counselor . . ."

"You aren't much of a pilot, either," Taylor said.

The pilot gave her a look. "Hey, sweetie, I saved us, didn't I?"

"Yeah, you got the landing thing down. The flying part needs a little work." Eric laughed loudly and then he and Taylor high-fived each other.

"So, where are we?" Melissa said. She looked scared out of her mind. It was probably about the millionth time she had asked somebody.

"I, uh . . ." Captain Russell scratched his head. "Technically . . ."

Everybody leaned forward, waiting to hear the answer to the question they'd all been having for the last hour.

"Technically. . . I don't know."

"What do you mean?" Abby said. "What about the radio?"

"Don't you have to leave a flight plan with the airport or something?" Nathan said.

Other kids chimed in, registering their surprise.

Hello! Daley wanted to say. *Haven't you guys been paying attention? What's with all the surprise?*

"Whoa! Whoa! Easy!" Captain Russell said, holding up his hands to quiet the group.

"We're not gonna be here long, right?" Taylor said, blinking her long lashes.

Can you spell "clueless"?

"Look, the storm came outta nowhere. I tried going around it, but every way I turned, things kept getting worse. My compass went out, so I couldn't get a consistent heading. There's no MLS or ILS out here, my GPS is on the fritz, and my TCAS III is no help. So I'm vectoring—"

"What you're saying—" Eric interrupted. "—I'm putting this into technical terms—you got us lost."

Everybody laughed. Nervously. That was the one good thing about Eric. He'd say the stuff everybody was thinking, but that nobody else was willing to say.

"I kept us in the air! When the lightning hit one of the engines it must have torn open a fuel line. I had to put her down. You snot-nosed kids are lucky you had a pilot as good as me." He pointed out at the empty ocean. "A lot of guys would have had you swimming."

The thought of that sobered the group.

"So does the radio work?"

The captain held up the radio he had been carrying, the wires dangling down his arm. "Oh, it works. But it's gotta be in range of another radio." He paused. "It isn't."

"So that means we're real lost," Melissa said.

The captain didn't answer.

"But—" Taylor blinked, looked around. "We're not gonna be here long. Right?"

"Isn't there such a thing as a homing beacon?"

"Absolutely," Captain Russell said. "They're called EPRBs. Emergency Positioning Radio Beacons. Very nifty devices. Satellites can pinpoint their exact location. Down to a matter of feet."

There was a sigh of relief.

"That's great!" Daley said.

Captain Russell looked at her for a long moment.

Daley could feel her face falling. "What?"

The pilot smiled cheerlessly. "We ain't got one."

"Are you really a pilot?" Eric said.

Okay, now Eric was really starting to get on Daley's nerves.

"Look, it's okay," the pilot said. "I've been in worse

messes than this."

"That I believe," Eric said.

"I'm gonna head inland and take a look around."

"No!" Nathan said. "Bad idea. We should stay together."

"Yeah, dude," Eric said. "Didn't you watch *Scary Movie 3*?" Only Taylor laughed this time.

"For all I know there's a resort just past those trees."

"Uh . . ." Nathan said. "I really think—"

"I think he should go, too," Daley chimed in.

Nathan looked at her sharply. "What if he gets hurt?"

"And what if help is only a few yards away?" Daley said.

Nathan glared at her, pointed his finger. "As a matter of fact, I happen to know—"

"Hey! Children!" the pilot yelled. "Give it a rest. The decision's made."

"I'll go!" Jory said.

"Me too," Ian said.

"We'll be safe in a group," Abby said.

Daley smiled. "See?" she said to Nathan. "They'll be fine."

Nathan shook his head.

"I disconnected the power so there's no chance of a fire," the pilot said. "But don't touch nothing."

Abby, Jory, and Ian were standing in a row looking expectantly at the pilot. Daley wished she could feel as confident about the pilot's leadership as they obviously did. Daley had seen grown-ups mess things up too many times to trust that this guy would get them out of a jam.

"What?" the pilot said, looking at the row of kids.

"We're with you, sir."

The pilot gave them a sour look. "Oh, that's comforting."

Abby, Jory, and Ian conferred briefly, then started pulling on backpacks.

"What's with the packs?" the pilot said.

"Camping gear!" Abby said enthusiastically. "Who knows how long we'll be gone?"

"I do," the pilot said drily. "Couple hours, tops."

Abby, Jory, and Ian followed close behind the captain, keeping time with his stride. He stopped suddenly, looked back at them.

"Okay," he said, "now you're making me nervous."

"Hey, Captain Crunch!" Eric called. "When you get to the resort, grab me a sandwich. Corned beef on rye, hold the mayo."

"And a venti latte," Taylor chimed in. "Low fat."

They both laughed. Daley shook her head.

Captain Russell glared at them, then pointed his finger at the DeHavilland. "You take care of my plane. If there's nobody else on this island, that bird is gonna be the only thing standing between us and catastrophe."

Eric snickered.

"You think I'm joking, you punk?" the captain said. "Anything happens to that plane, we're in serious trouble."

Eric looked at him sullenly.

The pilot turned and started walking briskly toward the trees. He was wearing plastic flip-flops. Maybe Nathan was right. Maybe it wasn't such a good idea for the pilot to leave. He was going to get a thorn in his foot or get stung by some creepy jungle insect. Infection would set in and he'd get gangrene or blood poisoning and—well, and then they'd be in worse shape than ever.

"What could happen to the plane anyway?" Eric said. "It's already crashed. It's not like anything worse could happen to it."

"Um, well, as a matter of fact . . ." Lex said.

But before Lex could say anything else, Nathan shook his head. "Bad idea, wandering off into the jungle like that.

Bad, bad idea. We should be working together."

"We are working together," Daley said.

What am I thinking? Nathan doesn't know squat.

Lex cleared his throat. "Excuse me? Excuse me? Hey, guys, there's something you should know."

"Yeah, we'll see," Nathan said, still talking to Daley.

"Yes, we will." Daley glared back at him.

"Excuse me . . ." Lex said. "Excuse me."

"Not now," Daley said.

At the edge of the jungle, the pilot and the three campers walked past a big rubbery plant with huge leaves. The giant leaves swayed in the breeze. They were almost as big as Captain Russell. It reminded her of some TV show where the people got shrunk to the size of mice and were always in danger of getting stepped on or eaten by cats.

And then Captain Russell and the others were gone.

Daley wasn't sure why, but suddenly she had this feeling like they were never coming back. She felt goose bumps rising on the back of her neck. *Shake it off, Daley,* she thought. *Shake it off.*

But the feeling didn't go away. They were all alone now.

FIVE

Lex was frustrated. Nobody took him seriously. Just because he was younger than the rest of the kids, they treated him like he was a baby.

He looked out at the waves as they hit the beach, a nervous feeling washing through him. Were his eyes fooling him? He figured he'd better find out. Lex ran and took the piece of driftwood he'd gathered and stuck it in the sand. Then he walked five paces toward the trees, stuck another stick in the sand. Five more paces, another stick. It wouldn't take long, and he'd be able to see for sure. Then he'd have some hard data.

Then maybe the big kids would finally listen.

He watched the waves lapping at the shore, admired his handiwork for about five minutes. No doubt. It was happening, just like he'd predicted. This was not good. This was not good at all. He needed to let everybody know what was going on.

Over at the tree line Nathan and Melissa were talking

intently. At the plane, Daley was still busy inventorying things, probably too full of herself to listen. Eric and Taylor were goofing around in the water again like little kids. They were pretty much useless. What about this guy Jackson? He was a little scary. Still . . . Something had to be done. Maybe he'd listen.

Lex walked over to Jackson, who was listening to his mp3 player in the shade, his eyes closed.

"Excuse me," Lex said.

Jackson didn't move.

"Excuse me! There's something I need to tell you about. We've got a serious problem here and nobody is listening to me."

Jackson didn't move. He obviously wasn't listening either.

Lex prodded the older boy with the toe of his shoe. Jackson opened one eye impassively, looked at Lex for a moment. He seemed unimpressed. Jackson's eyes closed.

"Fine, don't listen! But don't blame me when it happens!"

Nathan and Melissa sat in the shade watching Eric and Taylor splash around in the water.

"I'm really scared," Melissa said. "We're totally stuck here, aren't we?"

Nathan nodded.

"You think there are sharks out there?" Melissa said.

"Doubt it," Nathan said. "Not the kind we'd need to worry about." Down on the beach Eric chased Taylor into the water. Taylor tossed her long blond hair and shrieked. "Are they in denial or what?"

"It's weird to think you went out with Taylor," Melissa said.

"I know, I know," Nathan said sheepishly.

"She is so not your type." Melissa flushed. "Is that mean of me to say?"

"No, no, you're right. At first I thought she was cool. I liked how she dotted her *i*'s with little footballs."

"Seriously? Taylor likes football?"

"Well, no. Turns out she was trying to draw little flowers. They just looked like footballs because she can't draw. Oops."

Down at the shoreline Taylor looked up toward the trees. It was so yummy out here. The water was perfect. Mel and Nathan were moping around up in the shade. What was their problem? This was practically the coolest thing that had happened in her whole life. She imagined telling the girls on the cheerleading squad about it when they got home next week. They would be so envious.

Eric scooped up some water and splashed her. Taylor yelled and ran away from him. After a minute of splashing around, she and Eric crashed into each other and fell down on the sand. Eric had obviously aimed to make it happen— one of those accidentally-on-purpose things. And she let it happen. Hey, why not? There wasn't anything else to do. And he was amusing enough. For now.

She found herself looking up to where Nathan and Mel were talking again. When she looked back at Eric, she could tell he had been watching her eyes. He was totally into her. Of course, most guys were. But Eric more than others. She wasn't quite sure what she thought of him. Back at school? No, Eric wasn't the kind of guy she'd want to hang out with. But here? Here, everything was different. It was like being at summer camp. You didn't have to worry so much about what people thought of you because it would all be over soon. Here, it was just nice to have somebody who worshipped you. And who wasn't all serious all the time. Daley and Nathan—God, they were so competitive, it made you want to gag.

"It's weird to think you went out with Nathan," Eric said. "He's not your type."

"Please. Don't remind me. He's so boring. He kept talking to me about football . . . like I cared."

Eric looked up and down the spectacular deserted beach. Out at sea the storm was nothing but a memory, the dark clouds replaced with a sky that was so pure, so blue that it was hard to believe. "Is this not just totally the greatest thing that's ever happened in your life?"

Taylor smiled brightly. "I was thinking *just* the same thing. God! How cool is that?"

As she expected, Eric looked pleased and flustered at the same time. He leaned back in the sand and closed his eyes. "Sometimes I take a moment out of the day, just some little tiny moment, and I try to remember it so I'll have that moment for the rest of my life. Every detail. Do you ever do that?" he said.

It seemed like a totally dumb thing to do. Why would you care? "Omigod!" Taylor said. "I totally do that all the time!"

Eric smiled, pushed his straw hat forward so the sun wasn't in his eyes. "I'm gonna remember this moment forever," he said. "The clouds, the feel of the sun on my face, the wind against—"

"Psyche!" Taylor said, holding up her thumb and index finger, making the L-for-loser sign.

Eric sat up sharply, then grinned. "Oh, you suck!" He lunged at her, but she jumped up and ran off laughing into the surf. She threw her head back and let the warm water cascade through her hair.

Taylor smiled to herself. Yeah, she could have some fun with Eric. For the moment. For as long as they were stuck here. Which wouldn't be that long anyway.

Melissa stood up. She felt bad watching Daley work over by the plane. She hadn't rested for a single second since they hit the ground. Melissa felt tired just watching her. "Let's go see if she needs some help, Nathan."

Nathan rolled his eyes but then followed her as they walked over to where Daley was busily moving boxes around.

"Guarding the plane for Captain Russell?" Nathan said.

Daley looked up as they approached. "Just trying to get organized," she said. "Everything we have is in this plane. But it's all jumbled up. And since we didn't pack the camping supplies and stuff, we don't even really know what's here."

"Mm-hm," Nathan said.

"Captain Russell's not exactly an inspiring leader," Daley said. "But he's right about protecting the plane, you know. If it takes a while to find us, we're gonna need everything this plane's got."

Nathan slapped the metal side of the plane. "What's it gonna do, blow up? Fly away? Chase Captain Russell into the jungle because it misses him so much?"

Daley ignored his sarcasm. "Speaking of Captain Russell," Daley said, "as long as he's gone, somebody's gotta be in charge. I think it should be me."

"I bet you do," Nathan said.

Nathan was normally a really sweet guy—hey, he was Melissa's best friend after all—but ever since he'd lost the presidential election in school last week, he'd been bad-mouthing Daley nonstop. Melissa didn't want to say anything about it because she didn't want to make him feel bad . . . but she kind of wished he'd find another topic of conversation.

"Captain Russell will be back soon," Melissa said,

trying to make peace. "Why don't we just let him take care of things?"

"We tried that once and look where that got us," Daley said, pointing to the wrecked aircraft. "Besides, he's not here now."

Nathan looked around, like he had suddenly been struck by some kind of idea. He frowned, then went into the plane. He seemed to be looking for something. Daley watched him go. As soon as he was out of earshot, she leaned toward Melissa and said, "Until Captain Russell gets back, we need leadership. Can I count on you?"

Melissa hesitated. Before she had a chance to answer though, Nathan came back out of the plane.

"Hey, I'm gonna go look for water. Who wants to come?"

"I will," Melissa said.

"No, she's helping me set up camp," Daley said.

"But we need water," Nathan said.

"We've got plenty of bottled water."

"What if it runs out?"

"Then we'll deal. Right now we've got to get prepared to spend the night."

"Fine, yeah, whatever." Nathan turned to Melissa. "You coming, Mel?"

Melissa felt torn. She had to agree with Daley that right now having some shelter for the night was job number one.

"I told you," Daley said, "she's helping me."

Melissa tried to think of a way out, but she was sort of stuck. She gave Nathan a weak smile, shrugged.

Nathan didn't say anything, just grabbed his pack and walked away.

Nathan felt kind of relieved to be by himself. Just the sound of Daley's voice drove him bananas. Like she was the only person in the world who'd ever had a good idea. And what was up with Melissa, backing Daley's play like that? Well, if Melissa wasn't going to be his ally, maybe he'd find somebody else.

Taylor and Eric were lying on the sand sunbathing. He could hear their loud chatter. It was amazing. They were acting like they didn't have a problem in the world.

"If we're going home early, I'm going with a tan," Taylor said.

Eric grabbed the suntan oil. "Here, let me rub that on you."

"In your dreams." Taylor smiled. That smile that had seemed so bewitching to Nathan just a few months ago— now it seemed kind of, well, empty. Maybe even a little calculating.

"I'm going to look for fresh water," Nathan said to them. "Anybody want to come?"

"What for?" Eric said. He lifted his bottle of water above his mouth, squeezed out a stream. Half the water splashed out onto the sand. Nathan winced. "Hey, we got plenty," Eric said.

"Relax, Nathan," Taylor said. "We're not gonna be here long."

Eric gave Nathan his usual sly, jokey smile. "Dude, you're blocking my sun."

Nathan shook his head sadly, walked off into the jungle. The minute he got off the beach, he had the feeling of being very alone. All he could hear was the sound of the surf booming against the sand. No airplanes, no cars, no cell phones beeping. Man, they wanted eco-camping, and they were getting it!

He pushed his way through a bunch of tropical vegetation. The plants here were all rubbery-looking things with giant leaves. How did you go about finding water in a place like this? Look for a stream or something?

He kept wandering around, but the only water he found was a small swampy area full of green, slimy water. It pretty much looked like an instant case of diarrhea. Better give that a miss.

After a while Nathan realized that he couldn't hear the surf anymore. *Uh-oh*, he thought. What if he got lost? Which way? He looked up into the air. The sun had been . . . *that way*? No, wait, if the sun was that way, then the shore must be . . .

He started feeling a little panicky. He was ready to be back with his friends, back at the plane, back in civilization. The jungle was confusing. No paths, no straight lines—just tangles of vegetation and spiderwebs and vines and . . . He was walking quicker now, bushes and sharp leaves slapping at his legs. Wait a minute, hadn't he just been here about five minutes ago?

He was conscious now of all kinds of noises that he hadn't noticed before. Something grunted off in the bushes. What was *that*? An alligator or something? Whatever it was, it sounded big. And unfriendly. And definitely not human.

He hurried on. Which way? Which way? Where was the plane? Okay, this was really not so cool anymore. How could he get lost when he hadn't gone more than . . . No, no "lost" was the wrong word. He was just . . . He tried to think of the right word.

Suddenly he wished he hadn't come out here by himself. If he'd just been a little nicer, Melissa probably would have come with him. And they'd be having a good time.

But instead, he had no idea where he was. And he was feeling more and more panicked. He started running through the low bushes.

Suddenly he heard the distant sound of Daley's sharp voice cutting through the air. "Lex, what are you *doing*? Stop messing with those sticks and come do some *work*!"

And peeping through the trees he could see the tail number of the plane, 29 DWN. Man, he'd have never thought that crummy old plane would be such a welcome sight. But there it was: civilization. He started running toward the aircraft.

But then he stopped. He'd actually wanted to do two things out here. One was find water. So far he'd struck out on that. But he also wanted to do another entry in his video diary. It would be good to do it out here where he could say what he was feeling without anybody listening in.

He set up the camcorder in the crotch of a tree, aimed it toward the spot where he would be standing, then hit the RECORD button.

Nathan

So.

Man, I thought this whole eco-camping thing would be exciting. But it's turned out to be more than I bargained for.

There's a lot to catch you up on. You remember that storm that was blasting when I did my first entry in the plane? Well, we got struck by lightning or something and the plane's engines caught on fire and we crashed. Now we're here. Wherever here is!

There're eleven of us on the island. The only adult is the pilot. And he and some of the kids just went out into the jungle to see if there's anybody out here. I tried to tell them that there's nothing here. But the pilot was not a real great listener. And now it's just me, Mel, Daley, Lex, and some others.

Now that I've been out here in the jungle a little bit, I gotta admit, I'm worried. Captain Russell and the other kids went out into this mess. I mean I probably didn't get two hundred yards from the shore and I was totally lost.

Anything could happen to them out there and we're gonna need to prepare to be self-sufficient. Most of these kids here have no experience with camping or woodcraft like I do and so I'm thinking that—oops, hold on—

"There you are!" Melissa said. "What are you doing?"

Nathan hurriedly turned off the video camera. "Nothing, nothing."

"Still want help looking for water?"

"Sure."

"I *see* the camera." Melissa gave him The Look. It was the look she'd been giving him ever since they were about five years old when she told him that she could see right through him. She lowered her head and raised one eyebrow. Nathan flushed. Busted. Good old Mel—sometimes it seemed like she knew him better than he knew himself.

Nathan held up the camera. "It's dumb. I thought it would be a good idea to make a diary of what's going on."

"It's not dumb." Melissa suddenly looked excited. "Maybe I'll do one, too!"

Nathan held out the camera. When Melissa put her hand on it, he didn't let go. "So. You know, if we're stuck here for a while, somebody's gonna have to be in charge. I'm thinking it should be me. You okay with that?"

Melissa blinked, her wide black eyes looking at him uncomfortably. She swallowed.

"What?" Nathan said.

On the beach Lex watched the third stick as it was engulfed by waves. The stick fell over, drifted gently into the beating surf. Lex felt his heartbeat quicken. If his calculations were correct, they were going to be in real trouble. Soon.

S┬X

Daley looked up to see Eric reach into one of the bins she had carefully packed. He pulled out a black plastic food pouch full of dried food. Daley had inventoried them and discovered that most of the food was on the other plane. If they ate a normal diet of three meals a day, they had enough for exactly two days.

"Hey! What are you doing?"

Eric gave her his surely-you-are-the-most-uncool-person-on-the-planet look and then put the corner of the bag between his teeth. "What does it look like? Lunch."

"You can't," Daley said. "That's gotta last."

Eric took the bag out from between his teeth. "Till when? Dinner? Gimme a break."

"Forget it. Nobody eats till we figure out how to ration it."

"Ration? Are you serious? This is vacation!" He put the bag up to his teeth again. Daley snatched it out of his hand.

He gave her an irritated look. "Hey! Whoa. Who put you in charge?"

Daley didn't answer. What was wrong with everyone? It was like they were living in some kind of fantasy world. She tried to be sympathetic, but it was hard. The truth was, most of the kids at Hartwell had never experienced a single second's adversity in their entire lives. They still thought that everything turned up roses, no matter what. Not Daley. Daley knew better. Daley knew how harsh the world could be.

Eric sighed loudly and shuffled away.

Daley put the food pouch back in the plastic bin. As she was about to close the lid, Jackson ambled up. She noticed that he was carrying a long, straight stick. He'd carved the end into a very sharp point. He reached out with the point of the stick, preventing her from closing the lid.

"Excuse *me*," she said.

Jackson speared the very same pouch of food that she had just confiscated from Eric, then turned and walked away with the food on the end of his—well, call a spade a spade—it was a spear. A weapon. Daley felt a shiver run down her spine.

"Are you people listening to me?" Daley yelled after him. "You can't eat that!"

But she might as well have been yelling at a wall. Jackson just walked away.

Daley looked over at Melissa. Melissa's eyes widened a little. "Okay, that was a little creepy," Melissa said.

Daley turned to look at Jackson, who was now sucking food out of the pouch. Out of the corner of her eye, she saw Eric snatch another pouch out of the bin.

"Put that back!"

Eric tore the corner of the pouch, spit it on the ground, then squeezed some food into his mouth. "Hey, this is decent.

I think it's some kind of chicken."

This was rapidly getting out of control. Daley closed the bin, leaned against it.

Taylor walked up, looked at Eric and said, "I am starved! What is that?"

"Camp food." Eric opened his mouth so you could see a bunch of gray food on his tongue. "Uh? Pretty good. There's a ton of it in that bin over there."

"Okay, gross! But whatever."

Taylor walked toward Daley. Daley kept her arms locked on top of the bin.

"No! We've got to ration."

Taylor gave Daley a look, curling her upper lip slightly. "What's your problem, Daley?"

Daley glared back at her. All that pretty-girl stuff might work on boys, but it meant nothing to Daley. She didn't budge. To her left she saw Jackson climbing up onto the plane. He just sat there munching contentedly on his camp food, looking down at her with amusement. Daley was furious.

Nathan and Melissa walked up.

"What's going on?" Nathan said.

"Daley's trying to starve us," Eric said, wiping a smudge of mushed chicken off his lip.

"I'm not," Daley said. "But we've got to conserve food."

"Says who?" Taylor said.

"Hey, guys," Nathan said. "Daley's right."

Typical Nathan—always trying to horn in and offer up his version of "leadership." Daley glared at him. "I can handle this, Nathan."

"Just backing you up," Nathan said innocently. She could see him scheming, though, trying his best to think of something that would make her look bad.

"I don't need backup, thank you very much," she said.

"Nathan, you aren't in charge here either," Taylor said.

"Nobody's in charge," Eric chimed in.

Lex walked up and poked Daley in the hip with his finger. "Um, Daley? Can I say something?"

Daley ignored her little brother. "Excuse me, Eric, but when we need comic relief, I'm sure I'll ask for your help. But in the meantime . . ."

Lex kept poking her side with his finger. She slapped it away.

"Hey, somebody's got to take the lead," Nathan said. "I wanna give it a shot."

"Great," Eric said, giving Taylor a sidelong look. "Another power grab."

Taylor and Eric started saluting each other and marching up and down like soldiers.

Daley ignored their pathetic antics. Nathan was the real problem here. "Lead?" she said. "Why you, Nathan? I'm the one who's been setting up camp while you're wandering around—"

Lex poked her in the ribs again. Daley slapped his hand away again.

"See that's the problem, Daley," Nathan said. "I'm thinking strategically here and you're piddling around making lists and neat little piles of junk. What if we're here for two weeks? How important will your little lists and your little piles be when—"

Poking. Poking. Poking.

"You guys!" Lex said. "I have something important to say."

"Would you *please* quit irritating me!" Daley said.

"Loosen up!" Eric said. "We're on va-freaking-cation!"

"This is so not fun!" Taylor said.

Melissa held up her hands in frustration. "You guys are making me very upset."

Suddenly Jackson vaulted off the top of the plane, landing right in the middle of the group. He slammed his spear down into the sand.

Everybody instantly fell silent.

"Okay," Taylor said finally. "Scary."

Jackson looked around coolly. "Lex wants to talk," he said at last.

"Whoa." Eric grinned, chicken sticking to his teeth. "He speaks."

Jackson looked at Lex.

Lex pointed to himself questioningly, looking surprised. Jackson nodded.

"Uh, thanks," Lex said to Jackson. Then he turned to the group. "I don't mean to interrupt, but we're about to have a big problem."

SEVEN

Lex

My name is Lex Marin. Daley's my big sister. Actually my stepsister. She's pretty nice, I guess. But it's frustrating being the youngest kid here.

Nobody listens.

I feel like that's my life story. Back before Mom and Dad were divorced, they seemed like they were mad and scared all the time, so they never listened to me. Now that Mom's remarried to Daley's dad—I don't know, Mom's always busy doing charity work and Daley's dad is working or away on business trips. And when I see my real dad—well, that's not so fabulous either.

Even at school nobody listens to me. They all think I'm this big geek because I read all the time, and because I know stuff about history and science and because I like taking stuff apart and seeing how it works.

Okay, so maybe I am a big geek. But I pay attention. I try to see what's going on around me. I try to figure stuff out. A lot of kids—it's like they never think. Not for a second. Even big kids.

Like today. Why is a ten-year-old kid the only person who can see what's really going on?

Lex felt awkward now that everybody was listening to him. He cleared his throat.

"I don't mean to interrupt, but there's something you should know. The plane is our life raft. Right? Besides our gear, there's a ton of stuff on board that we can use. Like first-aid kits and tools and spare lightbulbs and—"

"Yeah, yeah," Eric, the big sarcastic kid, said. "Real interesting. Why don't you go and play with your toys while—"

Jackson pointed his stick at Eric—who immediately put this fake, sick-looking smile on his face and said, "No, but I mean, sure, finish your thought."

Lex was starting to like this Jackson guy. He was a little scary. But he spent more time paying attention to what was around him than he did trying to impress everybody. Unlike certain other big kids Lex could name. Lex smiled at Jackson. Jackson's expression, however, remained unchanged.

"The plane itself can help us, too," Lex continued. "There's fuel and batteries. And when search planes come over, they'll see the plane before they see us."

"What's your point, Lex?" Daley said. She'd been tapping her toe impatiently.

"I tried to calculate exactly, but it's hard. The storm we flew through is only going to make it worse."

"Make *what* worse?" Taylor said.

Lex turned and pointed at the water. The waves were crashing on the beach. They weren't especially high or dangerous-looking. The reef out in the deeper water calmed the surf down a little. But they just kept coming. One of them engulfed his fourth stick. It toppled over and then slowly washed back into the surf.

"The tide's coming in."

Blank looks.

Lex turned and pointed at a bunch of driftwood and seaweed that ran in a jagged line between the plane and the tree line. "See all that junk? That's the high-water mark."

Nathan was the first one to get it. "That means when the tide comes in, the plane floats away." His eyes widened slightly. "With everything we need to stay alive."

"I put those sticks in the sand every ten feet," Lex said. "The tide's rising at about six inches a minute."

Daley stared at the waves, swallowed. "You're saying—"

"Yeah," Lex said. "Unless we do something fast, the plane will be gone in an hour."

EIGHT

"Captain Russell! Captain Russell!"

The jungle had gotten denser, darker, more forbidding as they hiked deeper into the island. Jory felt a spike of fear in her chest. She was starting to fall behind. She had short legs and was not the world's most athletic girl. And Captain Russell didn't seem in the mood to slow down.

"Captain Russell!" Jory called again.

The pilot turned around and glowered at her. "What!"

"Sir? Captain?" Jory tried to hurry, the backpack thumping against her back as she trotted toward the rest of the group. It had seemed like a good idea to go with the pilot. But now she was getting the feeling that they'd made a big mistake. "Sir, my feet hurt."

The pilot held up one foot, showing off his pink flip-flop. He waggled his dirty toes. "You think my feet are feeling real peachy right now, sweetheart?"

Jory started to cry.

"Oh, for pity's sake!" the pilot said. "It's not bad enough we're lost in a freakin' primeval jungle, now I got crying girls to contend with?"

Abby, however, smiled serenely at Jory. Abby never seemed bothered by anything.

"Take a deep breath," Abby said.

Jory couldn't seem to stop crying.

"Jory," Abby repeated. "Take a deep, cleansing breath."

Jory took a breath, feeling the air shuddering in her chest.

"Good. Now out. Let the bad feelings go. Again, a deep, cleansing breath."

Jory breathed a few times, in and out, in and out. Abby's calm black eyes made her feel better. Jory wished she could be like Abby. Beautiful and calm.

"Can we go now?" the pilot said.

"Uh . . ." The last member of the party, Ian, held up his hand slightly. "Uh, captain, did you just say . . . *lost* in the jungle?"

The pilot's lip curled slightly. "Look around you, kid. What do *you* think?"

Ian looked around. The trees above them were high and thick, shutting out most of the sun. It smelled like rotting vegetation. Something skittered through the dead leaves next to them—a very large insect.

Jory wished she hadn't come here. This was a scary place.

"Let's just go," the pilot said. He turned and plunged into the trees, Abby and Ian following. The direction he was going was shrouded in shadow. For a moment it seemed as though the other three hikers had suddenly disappeared. Jory stifled a sniffle and hurried to catch up.

An unusually large wave hit the beach and a tiny ripple of water rose up the sand, uncomfortably close to the tail of the plane. Daley felt her lungs constrict. For a moment it was almost like she couldn't breathe.

"So what if we lose the plane?" Taylor said.

Taylor's dopiness immediately freed Daley from her brief bout of panic. "Yeah, no problem," Daley said sarcastically. "It's only got food and water and shelter and pretty much everything we'll need to survive. But so what?"

"Yeah, but we're not gonna be here long," Taylor said, looking around at everybody. "I mean . . . are we?"

"We really have to do something," Lex said.

"You're sure we have an hour?" she said.

"Give or take."

Nathan turned to Daley and said, "Look, you've been figuring out what's in the plane and getting things organized. Why don't you get the most important things up past the high-water mark . . . while I save the plane."

"While you *try*, you mean?" Daley said. She was irritated by Nathan's obvious attempt to take charge of the situation. The problem was, he was right. She knew exactly what was in the plane and where it was. She was the one who had moved everything. Daley clenched her jaw for a moment, then pointed at Melissa and Taylor. "You and you," she said brusquely, "come with me." Then to Nathan, "Well? You just gonna stand there? Go. Save the plane."

She turned and walked toward the plane. Melissa followed, but Taylor didn't.

"Kinda bossy, isn't she?" Taylor said to Nathan.

"Go, Taylor!" Nathan shouted at her, pointing at the plane.

Daley suppressed a smile at Taylor's shocked expression when Nathan had yelled at her. She wasn't used to having guys tell her what to do.

"Eric. Jackson. Lex." Nathan pointed at the trees. "With me. There are vines up there that we can use to pull the plane."

The boys all began trooping toward the forest—Eric lagging behind, as usual.

Daley made a quick mental checklist. "Okay. Girls," she said, "first priority, food and water." She pointed to the bins that she'd been organizing. "And Taylor, don't be sneaking food out of there."

"I'm sure!" Taylor said.

Daley was pleased to see Melissa jump into the work immediately, grabbing a box that was too big for her and struggling up the beach with it. Melissa was a little disorganized, but she tried hard and she didn't complain.

"Second priority," Daley said, "shelter. Tents, bags, air mattresses. Third priority, lights and batteries. Fourth priority—"

Taylor sighed loudly. "Alright already!" She picked up the smallest box of food and began walking up the shore like she was on a fashion runway, waggling her hips.

Daley wanted to scream.

Nathan and Jackson were the only ones who had brought decent knives, so they had to cut all the vines. Nathan had a custom-made hunting knife made by a famous bladesmith from Georgia. His father had given it to him when he made Eagle Scout. It was one of his proudest possessions. Jackson's knife looked like it was about a million years old, with duct tape wrapped around the handle. But Nathan could tell it was razor sharp.

"Eric, Lex—you guys find good vines and pull them off the trees. Jackson and I will cut them and drag them down to the shore. Jackson, make sure they're at least forty or fifty feet long. They won't do us any good if they're only ten feet long."

Jackson gave him a wry salute.

There was a feeling of excitement in the air. Everybody was working. Despite the heat and the mosquitoes, it felt like this was the first time that everybody was rowing in the same direction. Nathan felt a swelling of pride. He was pulling the team together now. Everybody was getting it, finally.

"Here!" Eric yelled. "I got a good one!"

Yes! Nathan smiled, surveying the busy team. *I am working it now.*

Eric yanked hard on the vine. Apparently he hadn't paid much attention to where it was going. The vine ran right behind Nathan's legs. It wrapped around Nathan's ankles, and his feet flew out from under him. He went down hard, slamming into the ground.

Eric looked away, pretending he hadn't done a thing.

Nathan stood up slowly, feeling a little stunned. "Nice!" he said.

Eric turned around, eyes all wide and innocent. "What?"

Most of the waves were now reaching the tail section of the plane. The DeHavilland Heron was in no danger of washing away at this moment—but Daley was surprised at how quickly the tide moved.

Taylor stepped out of the plane carrying several magazines—*Seventeen, InStyle, Glamour.*

"We are so gonna need these," she said, kissing the magazines. Melissa ran by her into the plane and then came struggling out carrying a tent and two sleeping bags.

Daley chose to ignore Taylor for the moment. Lex had

returned from the jungle dragging a pile of vines.

Daley ducked back into the hatch of the plane, came out with an armload of backpacks. When she hit the ground, her shoe got wet. This was going to be tight. There was still a lot of stuff to get out of the plane. She wasn't sure they'd make it.

Daley lugged all the backpacks up to the trees, where she found Taylor sitting on a box.

"What are you doing!" Daley said.

Taylor looked up innocently. "Inventory."

"Get up!"

Taylor looked over at Melissa like, *Is it just me?*

Nathan, Eric, and Jackson arrived at the pile of boxes, each dumping an armload of vines onto the ground.

"I'm already sick of this place," Eric said as he dropped his vines. "Tell me that's enough."

Nathan was glad to see that Lex had already managed to get a piece of real rope attached from the plane to a tree. He was a little nervous about these vines.

Lex must have read his thoughts, because the first thing he did was pick up a vine and pull on it. The vine snapped in two.

Nathan gulped. This was not cool.

Eric sighed loudly. "If you're about to tell me I just wasted the last hour breaking my back . . ."

"Hold on," Melissa said. "I bet we can fix that."

She picked up three vines and started braiding them together.

"Try that," she said, handing the braided vine to Nathan. He yanked on it as hard as he could. It held!

"You're a genius, Mel," he said.

"Who says home ec is useless?"

Taylor looked over Melissa's shoulder. "What's so special?

I've been braiding my hair since I was two."

Nathan handed her the three vines. "You're on."

Taylor looked irritable for a moment, then looked back at the plane. A wave hit the rear of the plane, sending up a spray of water. "I guess we'd better," she said.

"Okay, people!" Nathan clapped his hands. "Let's start stripping all the leaves off. Mel, you and Taylor start braiding."

For the first time, nobody had to be urged to work. Daley continued to pull things out of the plane and pile them up on the sand. Nathan almost felt sorry for her. He hated to admit it, but she was working like a dog, really getting a lot accomplished.

He set to work, tearing leaves off the vines. Within ten minutes, they had four or five long braided vines ready to go.

And they needed them. The plane was beginning to rock gently in the waves.

Daley dumped several bags on the sand and then fell down in a heap. After a moment she looked up and saw Nathan watching her. "Done!" she yelled. "The important things are out."

"Way to go!" Melissa called to her.

Lex grabbed one of the vines and headed out into the water.

Nathan's heart sank. He could see that they wouldn't reach all the way from the trees to the plane. "They're too short," Nathan said.

"No they're not," Lex yelled back to him. "Somebody help me. Tie them to the wings."

"And then what?" Nathan said.

"Then we surf."

Nathan frowned. What was the kid talking about? But then he figured that Lex had been right about everything so far. He probably had a plan.

"You heard him," Nathan called. "Let's get those ropes tied!"

Lex ran along the line of driftwood and seaweed that denoted the high-water mark, jamming sticks into the sand. "This is how far we need to pull it, everybody," he called. "Once we start pulling, we have to go until we hit the sticks."

Daley got up and climbed up onto one wing. Jackson climbed onto the other. Eric threw Jackson two of the braided vines, and Melissa threw the others to Daley.

The plane was shifting several feet with each wave now. Daley and Jackson tied furiously, then they both sprang off the wings at the same time.

"Grab the ropes and pull," Daley called.

Nathan grabbed a rope, pointed toward the other side of the plane. "Jackson! Over there. If we have all the strong people on one side, we'll just spin it around."

Jackson splashed through the surf to the other side of the DeHavilland.

"Pull!" Daley yelled. "Pull!"

Nathan hauled on the vine with all his might. He could feel the muscles in his back and shoulders bunching up until they felt like they'd burst. The plane, however, didn't budge.

"Pull!" yelled Daley.

"No," Lex called back to her. "Not yet. We're wasting our time. Everybody wait for the next big wave. Let the wave take it."

"Isn't that what we *don't* want?" Eric said.

The plane suddenly shifted as the last wave ran out, sucking the aircraft backward several feet.

"Ow, ow!" Taylor yelped.

Melissa stumbled and fell.

The plane was pulling them all deeper into the water. And they seemed powerless to stop it.

"Wait!" Lex called. "Wait!"

"You sure about this?" Daley said.

The plane bobbed in the water, then shifted out even farther.

"Lex, we can't hold it!" Nathan yelled.

"Wait . . ." Lex had let his braided vine go slack in the water. He wasn't even pulling. He was just looking out at the water. "Wait . . ."

"For what?" Taylor said. She was still pulling desperately, her tanned body angled so far back that her hair was hanging into the water.

"For . . . *that!*" Lex called.

A huge wave rocked the plane, almost overwhelming it. For a minute Nathan thought the plane was lost. But then it rose up out of the wave like a breaching whale.

"Now!" Lex yelled.

"Pullpullpullpull!" Daley yelled.

Nathan drove his feet into the sand and hauled on the vine rope with all his might. Everybody else was pulling, too.

And suddenly, like magic, the plane began to ride the wave.

"Yeah!" Eric screamed.

"Pull!"

"Go, go, go!"

Nathan felt like he had never worked so hard in his life. The plane picked up momentum and began skimming across the water.

"Pull! Pull!"

Everyone was yelling now.

Finally the plane slowed. The line of sticks Lex had made to show the high-water mark was still about ten feet away.

"Almost there!" Daley yelled.

"One last pull!" Nathan said. "Everybody together. One . . . Two . . ."

"Three!" Daley yelled.

They all gave one last heave and the plane gently nosed past one of Lex's marker sticks.

"Woooo!" Eric yelled, pumping his fists in the air. "We did it!"

Everybody started cheering and yelling, staggering out of the surf and falling exhausted to the sand. Nathan gave Lex a high five, then rapped knuckles with Eric.

Daley hugged Lex. Melissa hugged Nathan.

"We did it," she said.

Eric hugged Taylor, who hugged him back briefly, then abruptly pushed him away. Eric turned to Jackson.

"Don't even think about it," Jackson said.

Everyone laughed.

Nathan leaned back in the sand, laced his fingers behind his head, and stared up at the blue sky, feeling the sun warm his skin. This had been a big test. And they'd come through. The plane was their lifeline. Without it, they would be in a really deep hole. Knowing what they'd done gave him the feeling that maybe they'd be able to do what it would take to survive out here.

Nathan noticed Daley looking at him. She plopped down next to him.

"Does everyone else get it?" Daley said. "How serious our situation is?"

"I don't know," Nathan said. "But saving the plane? This is huge. If we'd lost it . . ." His voice trailed off.

"Yeah, I know," Daley said. "It scares me to even think about it."

"We did it though, didn't we?"

She nodded, smiled. "Nice work," she said finally.

"Thanks. You too."

Suddenly she looked embarrassed, like she had opened up to him in a way she didn't really mean to. She stood up quickly, brushed the sand off her pants, and walked over to where Lex was standing. Then she started talking animatedly to her brother, making a big show of being all busy and serious about something.

Nathan leaned back into the sand, letting his tired muscles relax.

He had been lying there for a while feeling contented with their triumph over the ocean when out of nowhere a thought wormed its way into his head: *Where were Captain Russell and the other kids?* The sun was starting to move down toward the mountain on the far side of the island. Captain Russell had said his little expedition would be gone for a couple of hours, max. It had to have been five or six hours by now. Way too long.

Nathan had been up to the top of the dune and seen how far this island stretched. He'd also been deeper into the jungle than anyone else. He knew how quickly someone could get lost out there.

No, that was the wrong attitude to take. Maybe Captain Russell had found some people. Maybe that was what was taking so long. Maybe he was out there organizing a rescue party right this minute. For all Nathan knew, he might walk into camp in the next ten minutes, a whole bunch of local people in tow.

But then another thought began to creep into his head.

What if . . . Nathan thought. *What if something happened out there? What if they never come back?*

He sat up and looked around. "Where are they?" he said.

But nobody was listening.

Anyway, Captain Russell would be back any minute, and things would get better. Wouldn't they?

NINE

"Where *are* they?" Melissa said, looking into the trees.

"I think they're lost," Nathan said.

"Or maybe Captain Russell changed his mind," Daley said. "They had some food and water in their packs. Maybe he decided to head all the way across the island and see if there's anybody on the north shore."

Daley was feeling nervous and impatient. They needed to be *doing* something. But not knowing where Captain Russell and the others were made it a little hard to decide what should be done.

"How long have they been gone?" Eric said.

Melissa looked at her watch. "I don't even know what time it is. I'm still on Los Angeles time." She squinted at her watch. "But I guess it's been about six hours."

"I think we should go looking for them," Daley said.

Nathan pointed at the sun. "Daley, it's getting late. What can we do that Captain Russell can't?"

"I still think . . ."

"Come here," Nathan said. "I want you to come look at something."

Daley scowled. "Every minute we mess around is a minute that—"

"Just come with me."

Daley rolled her eyes. But then when Nathan started walking, she followed him. He walked down the beach and then started climbing up the big dune that rose from a point a few hundred yards down the beach.

"What?" Daley said.

"Indulge me," Nathan said.

Daley sighed loudly, then followed Nathan up the tall dune. Because of the looseness of the sand and the steepness of the dune, it took longer than Daley had expected. When they finally crested the dune, the island sprawled out before them.

Daley felt her heart rise into her throat. Somehow she'd imagined that the island they were on was small. Maybe a mile across or something. But this stretched out for mile after mile. And nothing was there but jungle. And impassible-looking mountains.

"You see any sign of people out there?" Nathan said.

Daley didn't answer.

"I didn't either," he said. "And you know how fast you could get lost out there?"

It was then—at that precise moment—that Daley finally realized it. All afternoon she'd been working like a dog, keeping herself occupied, keeping her mind busy. Why? To distract her from one simple and obvious fact: They were on their own. Totally on their own.

For a moment she wanted to scream and cry and fall down in the sand. She could feel her lower lip tremble.

Then she felt Nathan's eyes on her. No, she wasn't going

to give him the satisfaction. Not in a million years.

"I have something to say," she said.

Nathan looked at her curiously.

"But I need to tell everybody. Back at the plane."

She turned and started trudging down the dune.

Daley

My name is Daley Marin.

I guess it's no secret to people who know me that I'm a control freak. But you know what? I may only be a kid, but I know how the world works.

If you saw me on the street, you'd just think, "Well, there goes some nice girl from a nice school with nice parents and nice clothes and a nice car and she has plenty of money and everything's lovey-dovey and hunky-dory in her life." And in a way maybe that's true.

Dad is married to a nice person. I have a nice stepmother and a pretty decent stepbrother. We live in a nice house. I'm president of my class at a really good school. All my teachers tell me, "Oh, Daley if you just keep your grades up, you're a lock to be valedictorian. You can go anywhere you want to college, and blah blah blah blah blah." Easy street, right?

But guess what? It wasn't always that way.

When I was in seventh grade, I came home from school one day and there was an ambulance sitting outside my house. I don't know exactly what happened. But my mom had fainted or something and then called 911. By the time they arrived, she was fine. Or it seemed that way.

Two months later, she went into the hospital with cancer. She never came out.

Dad was trying to take care of Mom and do his work, and a lot of stuff got lost in the shuffle. For a couple months there, I took care of the house, washed Dad's clothes, made my lunch, and did a lot of other stuff that my dad didn't seem to have the energy to take care of.

For the last week that Mom was alive, Dad stayed at the hospital 24-7, not even coming home at night. And I stayed there in our house by myself. I kept the house clean. I figured out ways to get food, and I cooked for myself. I washed my clothes. I did my homework. And nobody besides me and my dad ever knew a thing.

After it was over, Dad came home and he put his arms around me and said, "Sweetheart, I'm so sorry. I'll never leave you alone again. I'll always be there when you need me."

But a part of me knew that it wasn't true. There's just some stuff that other people can't do for you. Sometimes you just have to do things yourself. Hey, I know what it's like to want to lie down and quit. I felt like that every day that my mom was in the hospital. But I kept going. Maybe some of these kids think you can just cry and fall on the ground and some grown-up will come along and save you. Not me. I know better.

All these other kids? They've had these cushy lives

and they just don't know. So I'm tired of hearing all the whining. They just don't know how bad it can get. They just don't know.

And that's why they need me.

"Okay, everybody, listen up," Daley called.

Eric and Taylor were piddling around over by the airplane, laughing about something.

"Hey!" Daley yelled. "Everybody. Now." She clapped her hands.

Eric and Taylor walked over, looking at her sullenly.

"Guys," Daley said, "here's our situation. This island's bigger than we thought. Captain Russell and the others? They could be gone for a while. They could be lost. They could even be—"

"What?" Taylor said.

"I think 'dead' is the word she's looking for," Eric said.

"Whatever," Daley said. "My point is, Captain Russell will be back, but maybe not quite as soon as we thought. It's a pretty big island. If we don't run a tight ship, we're going to run out of food and water, we'll get sick, we'll—"

"What she's saying," Nathan said, "is that things could get really bad."

Daley smiled tightly at Nathan. "I'm capable of articulating my own thought, thank you very much."

"*Exsqueeze* me very much, your majesty."

"My point is, it's time for us to choose a leader."

"Exactly," Nathan said. "And I think, being modest about it, that I should be the one."

Daley stared at him. "Nothing personal, Nathan, but it's obvious *I* should be the one."

Nathan

Well, it's on. Daley and I agree on one thing: We need a leader. Hey, I'm willing to step up to the plate. But Daley thinks it should be her. I mean, sure, she gets stuff done. But at what cost?

She's so ... annoying! Being a leader is not just about shouting orders. You have to make people want to do stuff. I'm good at that. People like me. I don't have to yell.

Daley? Nah, forget it.

Melissa was suddenly feeling nervous. Nathan had really had his feelings bruised when Daley beat him in the presidential election in school last week. And now it seemed like he was all ready to get into it with Daley. Melissa wished everybody could just keep their voices down. Wasn't it bad enough that they'd just crashed on some deserted island?

"Look," Nathan said, "Captain Russell may not get back with help tonight. So it's obvious the first thing we need to do is make a fire. It'll be a signal for searchers and give us heat and light tonight, so—"

"Tonight?" Taylor said. "We're not staying the night, are we? I mean, *are* we?"

Daley ignored her. "Making a fire is a waste of time," Daley said. "If we're going to spend the night, we've got to make camp somewhere that's safe and sheltered."

"Hello?" Taylor said loudly. "I am *not* spending the night here."

Nobody even looked at her. She stood and walked away

in a huff, swinging her hips and flipping her hair and doing her best to attract the maximum amount of attention.

"Any chance she's not as clueless as she acts?" Eric said.

Daley and Nathan ignored him, glaring at each other.

"Job one," Nathan said. "Fire."

"No, we find a camp, *then* we worry about fire."

Melissa looked back and forth between them. "Any chance we could sort of work on *both* things? I mean, wouldn't that—"

Nathan cut her off. "Look, Daley, I know about these things," Nathan said. "In my great-great-grandfather's book he says right there in the very first chapter that fire is one of the five most important—"

"Oh, here we go again," Daley said. "My great-great-great-great-great-great-grandfather, the famous explorer. You may recall he explored the *North Pole*? Something tells me that fire's a little more important there than it is here in our tropical paradise."

"We need fire."

"First a campsite."

"Fire."

"Camp."

"Fire!"

"Camp!"

Melissa felt like sticking her fingers in her ears. This whole thing was getting too intense.

Nathan and Daley glared at each other for several seconds, then Daley turned to her little brother and said, "Lex, you come with me. We're finding a campsite."

"Okay."

"Melissa, you too."

"How many people do you need?" Nathan said. "Or maybe you don't trust your own gut."

Melissa looked nervously from one to the other. "Uh . . . maybe I should help Nathan start a fire," she said.

"Fine!" Daley said. "I'm sure he'll need it."

Melissa turned to Eric. "And I guess maybe you can gather some firewood?"

Eric raised one eyebrow. "Gee, thanks, Melissa. I'll get right on that." He adjusted his straw hat, then sauntered toward the trees.

"Don't burn down the jungle!" Daley called as Nathan and Melissa began walking away.

"Don't get lost!" Nathan called back.

As Melissa turned to look back, she noticed that Jackson had separated himself from the group. He was sitting up against a palm tree, watching everybody with a look on his face that seemed half amused and half disgusted. He shook his head, then sat back, put his earbuds in, closed his eyes, and cranked up his tunes.

Melissa watched him for a moment, feeling a brief stab of envy. He seemed so unconcerned, so detached from everybody else's problems. She wondered what it would feel like to be so calm and confident.

Melissa

Boy. What a bad start. First Captain Russell walked off and left us. I mean, I'm sure it was the right thing to do. He's a grown-up and everything—I know he knows what he's doing. But it just makes me nervous having to sit around waiting for him to come back with help.

And now it's looking like he's going to be longer than he said he'd be. We're kind of going to have to

get organized all by ourselves. We could be stuck
here for a while. I mean, we're just kids. We could,
like, starve or something if Captain Russell doesn't
get back soon. I guess we were all relieved once we
landed because it was like . . . hey, we're still alive! But
now I'm . . . I'm kinda getting scared again.

We needed to come together today. If Captain
Russell doesn't bring help and we can't figure out
how to get along, then we're gonna be in big trouble.
But Nathan and Daley couldn't agree on anything.
It's bad enough we're marooned here. But now
everything's getting all tense and weird.

And then I totally made things worse.

"I mean, what's *with* her?" Nathan said. Melissa was
following along after Nathan, her arms full of driftwood.
"Daley's bossing everybody around like we're idiots."

Melissa stooped to pick up a piece of wood.

"Hey, Mel, think!" Nathan said. "That wood's totally wet.
We need dry stuff."

"Sorry." She felt like saying, *Look who's talking.* But then,
that would have been kind of harsh. Melissa didn't like
saying bad things to anybody.

"You're on my side, right, Mel? I mean we need to be
like a team, you know."

"Of course I'm on your side. But I think it's important that
we all listen to each other and—"

Nathan interrupted her. "Exactly! Tell Daley that!"

On the beach, Eric had dropped his small load of

firewood, and was now digging a hole in the sand while Taylor watched. He shaped the piles of sand carefully, making the hole longer.

"Perfect," he said finally. He was pretty pleased with himself. It was like a beach chair. Except made out of sand. "Check it out."

Taylor walked over and looked at the hole, then spread her towel inside and lay down, smiling contentedly. After a moment, her smile faded. "Poo," she said.

"Poo?"

"Bad angle." She turned and squinted up at the sun, holding one hand up in front of her face. "Could you dig another one facing more this way."

It wasn't really a question, the way she said it.

But Eric didn't mind, not really. Hot girls were always a little high-maintenance, right?

"Sure," he said. "How about right here?"

Taylor leaned back and closed her eyes without looking where he was pointing. "I'm sure it'll be fine."

Eric felt a little surge of excitement. See? She trusted him. Once a girl trusted you, you could pounce like a tiger on a helpless fawn. Or something like that, anyway. He smiled to himself.

Daley and Lex looked around the clearing. It was a small circle of grassy land in the middle of higher trees. The sunlight came through the limbs, marking the ground with dappled sunlight. It was very pretty.

Daley dumped her heavy load of camping gear and smiled.

Lex poked the ground with his toe. He didn't like what he felt there.

"Perfect," Daley said brightly. "It's a perfect spot to make camp."

Lex tried to be diplomatic. "Hmm. You know there's a lot of factors to think about. We want to be close to the beach but safe from the tides. It's got to be protected from rain and sun but not have a lot of bugs and mold that would ruin the food. And then there's the chance of animals coming by and—"

"Alright, whatever," Daley said. "Is this perfect or is this perfect?"

"Well . . . no."

"No!" Daley frowned at him. "Then where do you think we *should* camp?"

"Honestly?" Lex was a little nervous saying it now that they'd been lugging this junk all over the place. "Honestly—back at the airplane."

Daley cocked her head forward and gave him her patented I'm-big-and-smart-and-you're-just-a-punk-kid look. Then she sat on the ground, leaned her back against the tent bag, and said airily, "Well, I happen to think it's perfect."

And Lex knew her well enough by now to know that she wasn't going to change her mind.

Nathan dumped his armload of sticks on the ground near the airplane, gave a disgusted look at the tiny pile that Eric had gathered, and then put it out of his mind. You couldn't control everybody. This was going to be fun. He'd read in his great-great-grandfather's book about how to make fire when you didn't have matches.

"There's an excellent diagram in my great-great-grandfather's book about how to make fire. He was in the cavalry in the late 1800s fighting Indians in the Dakotas once, and they got chased through this river. Everybody's matches got wet and they lost the pack horses that were carrying their flint fire strikers. This big snowstorm was whipping across the prairie, and he knew they needed a fire or they'd freeze. So he used this method shown to him by a Lakota Sioux warrior."

Nathan started making a little pile of straw. Then he searched for a piece of wood until he found what he needed. "Perfect!" he said. "Check this out!"

This was going to be totally cool. The book showed everything he needed to do.

"See, Mel?" he said. "You rub back and forth in this little channel . . ."

"I thought you sort of twiddled it between your palms so it rotates in a—"

"Yeah, well, that's one way. But the book says this works better. More motion means more friction. More friction means more heat."

Nathan rubbed the point of the stick vigorously back and forth in the channel. "I wish this wood wasn't so soggy."

"Maybe we should put it out in the sun and let it dry?" Mel said.

Nathan was eager to get the fire going. Some kind of little victory like that would get everybody's spirits up.

"Nah, I want to get this going."

"What about matches?" Melissa said.

"Uh . . ." Nathan looked up. It hadn't occurred to him. "Well, yeah, okay, why don't you check the gear just in case." He gave her a sheepish smile. Kinda obvious, wasn't it?

Melissa headed off toward the plane. Nathan continued to rub the stick back and forth. After a minute, his arms started getting a little tired. Not a lick of smoke. He stopped, looked at the wood. Okay, so Mel had been right. This piece was kinda wet. Maybe he'd try another one. He started combing through the pile, looking for something drier.

Taylor looked over at Eric, who was staring out at the ocean. She was getting thirsty but didn't really feel like getting up.

"What ya looking at?" she said.

"Water. Lots of water. No rescue boats, no airplanes. No nothing. Just a whole lotta wet."

She leaned over at him, knowing he'd look at her. He did as she expected, running his eyes down her body.

"You know, Eric," she said, giving him her big-eyed look, "you're the only one I trust here."

Eric cleared his throat. "Really?"

"Sure. You're the smart one. While everybody else is running around pretending to be important, you're sitting here saving your strength." She wondered if she was overdoing it a little. But then, that's what people expected from her. She put her hand on his arm. "That's very clever, Eric."

Eric was obviously eating it up. Sometimes the dumb stuff boys would believe if you just flirted hard enough amazed her. "Yeah," he said. "I guess it is."

"You're funny, too. The good kind. Usually. When we get home, I can definitely see us hanging out." In his dreams!

"Oh, man, I've been wanting to ask you out ever since that day in chorus when you fainted. Remember that? You were so . . . sweaty."

Okay, creepy. She smiled at him anyway. "I think as long as we're here, you and I are going to have to rely on each other."

Eric about broke his neck nodding. "Absolutely." He put his hand on her hand. She slowly extricated it from his grip. It was fine flirting with a guy. But there were limits. He could be amusing, sure. And all his sneaky little schemes could probably be useful to her. But she couldn't let him get the impression that he could start pawing all over her!

"We think the same, Eric."

"I completely agree."

Taylor smiled and leaned back in her "chair," gave it a few seconds, then acted like she'd just been struck by a sudden idea. "Hey, you know what? Why don't you go to the plane and get us a couple waters."

"Okay!" He hopped up, then suddenly got this guilty look on his face. "Oh, no, bad idea. Daley'd have a cow."

Taylor gave him her pouty, I'm-so-disappointed-in-you face. "I'm thirsty, Eric." She shrugged, then looked away from him. "But then if Daley's more important to you than I am . . ."

"Hey, now look . . ."

"I mean, you wouldn't want me to faint again. Would you?"

"No, conscious is good."

"Anyway, Daley's blowing this whole thing out of proportion. Captain Russell's gonna walk out of those trees any minute with a bunch of rescuers and suddenly all this drama about water is gonna seem totally stupid."

"I'm sure you're right," Eric said.

She turned around and gave him her biggest, warmest smile. "Perfect!" Then she reached over and touched him on the toe with one manicured fingernail. "Make sure it's chilled."

Eric blinked.

Nathan rubbed the stick back and forth furiously. His arms were getting really sore now and there hadn't even been a puff of smoke.

He looked around to see if anybody was watching. They weren't. He ran back to the pile of belongings, pulled out his pack, and unzipped the back pocket. There was his prize possession, a 1924 edition of his great-great-grandfather's book. Nathaniel Edmund McHugh—Nathan's namesake—who had been one of the first people to travel by dogsled to the North Pole, and who was the first man to climb Margherita Peak, the third largest summit in Africa, and who . . . well, bottom line, he'd done a lot of cool stuff.

Nathan flipped through the book to the page about starting fires. There was a crude sketch of the tools and the sticks of wood required. He scanned the paragraph where his great-great-grandfather had talked about fire-starting. It seemed like he was doing everything right.

Avoid cottonwood and other similar "trash trees" of that nature, the text read. *The ideal wood is firm but pliable, hard but not brittle, and perfectly dry.*

Trash trees. What was a trash tree? For all he knew, every tree on this stupid island was a "trash tree."

Nathan

I mean, fire is important, sure. But it was more than that. It was a symbol of my ability to lead. I wanted to prove to everybody that I knew exactly what I was doing. There was only one problem. I had no idea what I was doing.

Nathan ran back and felt the tinder again. He whittled a stick and some shavings from a little branch. Had it been dry enough? He felt the tinder. Hm. Kinda damp. That had to be the problem.

Wait a minute! He had an idea. He threw the handful of tinder down, hopped up, and broke into a run.

Melissa was looking for matches. She had hunted through about eighteen boxes, a couple of backpacks, a fanny pack, two plastic tubs, and more bags than she could count. And so far . . . zilch. She was getting a knot in her stomach. She didn't want to let everybody down. She hadn't wanted to hurt Nathan's feelings, so she hadn't said anything—but she just wasn't sure that rubbing sticks together would get the job done. Most of the wood they'd found was either wet or crumbly or the wrong shape.

She was on her hands and knees now, yanking boxes out from under other boxes in the pile. Had she looked in this box yet? Or not? She couldn't remember.

Almost all the cooking stuff—lighters, fuel, camp stoves, matches—had apparently been packed in the other plane. She kept digging around, kept finding every camping item you could think of. Except matches. Suddenly she felt like crying. Oh, this was stupid! Getting all worked up over a few matches? It's just that—

She opened the box, looked inside. Amazing! There they were, matches!

Melissa grabbed the matches, waved them in the air, and did a brief dance—pumping her hips like, *Work it! Work it!* She felt more than a little silly when she noticed Eric watching her.

"Matches!" she said, explaining.

"That is so totally awesome!" he said. He gave her this big smile that she suspected was probably totally fake. But with Eric you never quite knew. "Really! I'm so happy for you, I'm gonna celebrate."

He walked by her, opened the cooler with the water in it, pulled out two full bottles.

"Keep up the good work, dude!" He held up one of the

water bottles like he was toasting her, then started walking back toward Taylor.

"Hey, wait!" she yelled. He didn't show any sign of hearing her. "You probably ... shouldn't ... take the ..." Her voice trailed off. Like anybody ever listened to her anyway, huh? She put the matches in the pocket of her shirt, ran after him.

Nathan arrived at the pile of their belongings. Melissa was just leaving, running after Eric and looking all flustered and excited. What was that about?

Well. Couldn't worry about Melissa right now.

He hunted through the pile. Ah-hah! There it was. He grabbed a copy of Taylor's *InStyle* magazine. Then, after a minute's thought, stuck it under his shirt. If somebody saw him carrying around a copy of a magazine for girls, he'd look like a total dork.

He headed back toward the place where he'd been trying to start the fire.

Daley lay in the grass, her back against the tent bag, looking up at the softly swaying trees. For a moment a feeling of peace came over her. Okay, so this was it. This was going to be home for a while. When you got used to the idea, it wasn't so bad.

Lex kept wandering around looking at things with this skeptical look on his face, wincing every now and then.

"Yeah, okay, I get it," Daley said finally. "You don't like the campsite. Come on, don't be a geek. It's perfect. There's tree cover so we won't get rained on too badly, but the sun still comes through enough to keep down the mold. It's big enough for a couple of tents. We can even build a shelf to keep things away from the animals."

"Like that twelve-foot crocodile over there?"

Daley whipped around. Of course there was no crocodile behind her. She scowled. "Ha-ha. You're a riot."

"Seriously, though . . ." Lex said.

"What is your problem? It's cool here. Inside that plane, with the metal skin in direct sunlight? It'll be about a million degrees." She felt the ground. "I think it's because the ground's a little moist."

"Which is my whole problem. We don't want to be living on damp ground."

"Why not? We'll be in tents."

"Tents get wet. We don't want to be lying on the damp ground."

"Why not?"

"Because things live in damp ground."

"Things? What things?"

"Critters."

Daley punched his arm, laughing. "Critters. Thank you very much for that. Specifically what critters?"

Lex scratched his face, bent over, peered at her leg. "Well . . . for instance . . . that." He pointed at her leg.

"What?" She rolled her leg over to see what he was pointing at. It took her a second to make sense of what he was squinting at. It looked like a piece of fungus or something— a gross black blobby sort of thing stuck to her leg.

"Oh God," she said.

Because finally she got it. It looked like a . . .

"It's a leech," Lex said, squinting intently at her leg. He seemed way too interested.

"Oh God. Oh God." Daley felt all weird in her stomach. She wanted to jump up and start running, but she was too freaked out to move. "Get it off! Get it off!"

"Don't wig out," Lex said. "It's only a leech."

"Only! It's disgusting." The leech rippled like a piece of black Jell-O. "Are they poisonous?"

"No."

"Thank God."

"They only drink your blood."

"Lex!"

"Relax. There's only one. How much blood can it get?"

Daley lifted her leg to get a closer look. As her leg moved, she realized there wasn't just one. There were two. No three. No ...

Oh God. Oh no. This wasn't happening. There were dozens of them. On both legs.

"Yeah. Hm." Lex looked curiously at the leeches. "That's not so good."

Daley couldn't help herself. Jumping to her feet, she screamed and began to run.

TEN

"Eric! Eric!"

Melissa was still trotting after Eric, who was walking jauntily back toward Taylor, carrying the two bottles of water.

"Eric, you're not supposed to drink the water."

"Why's that?" Eric had finally reached Taylor. He tossed her a bottle.

"Thanks!" Taylor said brightly. She uncapped it and took a long pull on the water.

"Guys!" Melissa said. "Daley hasn't figured out how to ration the water yet. And if we just start drinking it, then ..."

"Then what?"

"Well ..."

Eric shook his head sadly. "Listen to yourself. Why do you do everything you're told? Can't you think for yourself?"

"Well, sure, but—"

"But what? We came out here for an adventure. Look around you. This is an adventure. That doesn't mean we have to be all *Oh God the sky is falling everything's terrible life sucks oh it's so horrible* all the time." He pointed at the beach. "This place is *awesome*! Look at it."

"Yeah, but . . ."

"No! Look at it."

Melissa looked around for a minute. Eric was right. The beach was right out of one of those *Travel + Leisure* magazines that her mom was always reading.

"Dude," Eric said, "have you even gone swimming yet?"

Melissa felt silly. Practically a whole day on a beach and— other than when they were pulling the plane up the beach— her toes hadn't even touched the water. "Well . . ." she said.

"Captain Russell could walk out of those woods ten seconds from now with a whole rescue party. And guess what would happen then? They'd drag us off the beach, put us in some boat or plane or something, and we'd be on our way back to LA in about ten minutes."

"Yeah, but . . ."

"Think about it. Thirty years from now you'll be thinking about this one day. This'll be like the biggest thing that ever happened in your life. Are you gonna look back on it and go, *Gee, I was on that beautiful island for all that time and what did I do? I was schlepping camping equipment around. What a waste!*"

Melissa just stood there. Maybe he was right.

Eric looked at Taylor. "Taylor, I think she's afraid."

"I am not!" Mel said.

"Maybe not of swimming. But you're definitely afraid of having fun."

"That is *so* not true! I have lots of fun!"

"Oh yeah," Taylor said. "You're a regular national holiday."

"You want to see?" Melissa felt her cheeks getting flushed. "I can have fun! I like doing stuff! Watch!"

For a moment she thought about going back to get her swimsuit. But that would sort of ruin the moment. By the time she'd get back, Eric and Taylor would have practically forgotten the whole thing. She decided to make a statement.

She ran into the water, dove headfirst into a rolling wave. It tumbled her over, banging her into the sand. She stood up, spluttering and laughing, pulling back her wet hair. Man, it felt totally *great!* Eric was right. She needed to stop and smell the roses sometimes.

Up on the beach Taylor and Eric were talking about something—probably her—shaking their heads like they were watching some kind of really pathetic performance.

To heck with them! She lay on her back and did the backstroke. A wave crashed over her head. The warm water tugged and bubbled around her. Wow. This was the greatest. This was totally, totally the greatest.

Nathan walked by Eric and Taylor, still holding the *InStyle* magazine under his shirt.

"What are you guys doing?" he said.

Eric and Taylor looked up. Taylor thrust a nearly full bottle of water into Eric's hand. He tried to hide it. "We're watching Melissa get crazy," Eric said.

"I saw that water, dude," Nathan said.

"Huh?" Eric and Taylor both tried to look all innocent.

Nathan laughed. "Hey, I don't care. Daley's the one keeping track of the supplies. I'm doing fire."

Melissa ran up out of the surf. "That was awesome!" she yelled. Water streamed from her clothes. "You gotta go in, Nathan."

"I will. Soon as I get the fire started." Nathan could feel the magazine getting a little sticky against his chest. Which reminded him . . . "So, hey, did you find any matches?"

"Yeah," Mel said.

Nathan grinned. Thank goodness. He felt a flood of relief. Sitting out there rubbing on all that wet wood, he'd started feeling a little desperate. Now he wouldn't have to make a fool of himself trying to start a fire by rubbing some junky, wet twig on some junky, wet piece of wood.

"I . . ." Mel blinked.

"What?"

Mel patted the left pocket of her wet pants, then the right, then the breast pocket of her dripping flannel shirt. Her face fell.

"Uh-oh," Eric said, grabbing Taylor's arm. "Party's over."

He and Taylor jumped up and started tiptoeing away in an exaggerated manner.

Melissa reached into her shirt pocket, pulled out a book of matches. They were completely soaked. She tore the pack open. The little red tips of the matches were wet and crumbling.

Nathan felt sick. "But . . . there are more, right?"

"No," she said quietly. "This was it." Holding up the ruined matches.

Nathan's shock turned to anger. How could she do this? "You're telling me you just ruined the only matches we had?"

"I . . . I'm sorry."

"Sorry? Sorry! Tell everybody you're sorry while we're freezing tonight. Tell everybody you're sorry when . . ." Nathan clapped himself on the forehead. This sucked. "Mel . . . you're the one person I thought I could trust. The *one* person! And now look at this!"

He grabbed the matches out of her hand and threw them furiously on the ground.

"Nathan, please. I'm so sorry!" Mel looked like she was

going to cry. Now he felt like a jerk. Well, what was he gonna do? He turned and stalked off.

Jackson stood under a palm tree watching him impassively.

"What!" Nathan said. "What are you looking at?"

There was something in Jackson's eyes that made Nathan wish he'd kept his mouth shut. He hurried away.

This was really not good at all. If Captain Russell didn't get back with help soon, they were gonna need fire big-time.

Please, please, please, he thought. *Let me get this fire started.*

ELEVEN

Melissa

I don't know how I could have been so dumb. I mean, Eric said I wasn't any fun, but that's not true! People always say that and it's not fair. He's so wrong. Not that I'm blaming Eric for what happened. It's all my fault. I let Nathan down and . . . oh man, I don't even want to think about what Daley's going to say.

I wish Captain Russell would get back. I'm starting to get really worried. He made it sound like he was just going to be gone for an hour or two. But it seems like it's been a lot longer than that. Am I being a wimp?

I don't know. I'm just so scared. Eric and Taylor seem to think this whole thing is just a game. And then Nathan and Daley are acting like we might be here forever. I just don't know who's right. All I know is—

Oh my God! Somebody's screaming. I'd better go.

Daley burst onto the beach running at full speed, screaming her head off. Lex pursued her.

"Stop!" Lex called. "Daley, stop!"

Daley was running out of breath. She halted in the sand, realizing there was nowhere to go to get away from the leeches. "Get 'em off! Get 'em off!"

She clawed at her legs, but the leeches were so slippery, she couldn't dislodge them.

"No!" Lex said. "Don't do that. Pulling them off is the worst thing you can do. Their pincers will get stuck under your skin and they'll get infected."

Daley stopped trying to get the leeches off. She was still shaking—but she had enough self-possession to realize that if she got a serious skin infection here, it could cause . . . Well, she didn't even want to think about what could happen then.

"What do I do, Lex?" she said.

"There're two ways to get rid of leeches. One way is to touch them with something hot. Like a burning stick."

"Fresh out of those," Daley said sharply.

"The other way is simpler."

"Tell me!"

"As soon as they get full of blood, they just drop off all by themselves."

The thought of sitting around waiting for a bunch of leeches to suck all her blood out turned Daley's stomach. She put her face in her hands. "Ugggghh."

"I think we need a fire," Lex said softly.

Nathan was still trying. But he wasn't getting anywhere. He got a tiny curl of smoke at one point, but then his arms tired out.

He heard someone crunching through the leaves and looked up. It was Eric.

"Hey, how's it going?" Eric said.

"You see fire?" Nathan was feeling irritated.

"Nope."

"That's how it's going."

Eric shuffled his feet back and forth awkwardly, his hands deep in the pockets of his pants. "Look, uh—it wasn't all Melissa's fault about the matches."

"No? Did somebody push her in the water?"

"No, not at all. I mean, it's just—she didn't mean to ruin the matches."

Nathan rubbed the stick a few times. It was digging a groove in the wood. "I know she didn't mean to. But she did." He looked up at Eric. "Thing is, man, we're in trouble. We can't be making bonehead moves like that."

"Right. No bonehead moves. Got it."

Nathan watched Eric wander away. Was Eric being sarcastic? Or was it finally sinking into his brain that this wasn't a party?

He took a deep breath, leaned into the work again. Maybe it would happen this time.

Melissa was back at the provisions pile, hunting through the boxes for about the fifth time. If there was one book of matches, maybe there were two. Maybe she'd just skipped over them the first time. And the second. And the third. And the fourth. And . . .

She felt a tear starting to run down the side of her face. She threw the box she was searching through onto the ground. Plastic bags full of dried food spilled all over the sand.

When she looked up, Jackson was standing there. She

pawed at her face, hoping he hadn't seen the tears running down her nose.

"Hey," he said softly. "Take a pause."

Melissa flopped down on the pile of sleeping bags. There must have been fifteen of them. They didn't have food or water or fire. But, boy, did they have sleeping bags.

"I am such a loser, Jackson."

"Says who? Nathan?" he said.

"He didn't have to. He's trying so hard, and I let him down."

Jackson sprawled down next to her, letting his arms splay out on the soft pile of bags. "Maybe it's time he took a pause, too."

"Would you help him? With the fire, I mean?"

Jackson shook his head. "Nah. There's already too much static. He'd take it the wrong way."

"Please. Help him."

Jackson stretched, stared up at the cloudless blue sky. He drummed his fingers on his thigh. Finally he stood up as though he'd made a decision.

Daley was trying a new approach. Maybe saltwater would get rid of them. She was hip-deep in the surf, moving around. Or, as Lex put it, she was "agitating" the leeches. She couldn't feel them now. Maybe they were gone! Of course they never did really hurt. She kept moving around for four or five minutes. Everybody who had gone for a swim had climbed out of the water all grinning and happy. The water didn't seem to have that effect on her, though. It just made her feel impatient.

Finally she burst out of the water, ran up on the beach. The leeches were still hanging from her legs. She felt a surge of disappointment.

"Are *any* of them gone?" she said to Lex.

He bent over and looked at her legs, pointing at them and counting. He had to count twice. Finally he stopped and said, "No. Every one of them's still there."

If anything, they were just getting bigger, slowly filling with blood. How much could she lose before it started affecting her?

As if in answer to her question, Lex said, "When the body loses more one-fifth of its blood volume, people normally lapse into unconsciousness. Then . . ."

"Forget it, Lex. I don't want to know." She put her face in her hands. "What am I gonna do?"

"If Nathan's got the fire started, we can use it to—"

"I don't want to use his stupid fire." She looked down at the leeches. "You know what? Never mind. I really, really want to use his stupid fire." She began walking toward the trees. "Come on, Lex."

Nathan

All my life I've been competitive. My dad's this famous lawyer. Seems like every time I open the paper, there's his picture, defending some famous person in court. And my mom? She's a pretty well-known opera singer.

I could tell you about other people in my family. They're all good at stuff. Not just their jobs. Good at everything. I mean, my dad plays saxophone and he's totally great at it. He could probably be a professional jazz musician if he wanted. My mom made the Olympics in the two-hundred-meter hurdles. My older sister is double majoring in fine arts and finance at an Ivy League school. She's already had paintings exhibited at a gallery in New York, and she's being recruited by every investment bank in the world. My uncle Burton is president of a university and a master-level bridge player, and my aunt Ruth is a black belt in karate and an internationally known mathematician and ... well, you get the point ...

I feel like a constant failure. I mean, I'm one of the best students at Hartwell. But not *the* best. I'm co-captain of the football team. But I'm not *the* best rusher or *the* best receiver or *the* best anything. I'm like Mr. Also-Ran.

My great-great-grandfather saved twenty-three cavalrymen from freezing to death in a blizzard in 1887. And I can't even start a fire.

What's wrong with me?

Nathan was wearing out. Back and forth, back and forth, back and forth with the stick. Eric was lounging around a few feet away.

"You ever think about doing the twiddle-it-between-your-palms method?" he said. "That's how they did it in that movie."

"Yes, I considered the freakin' twiddle-it-between-your-freakin'-palms method," Nathan snapped. "According to my great-great-grandfather's book, that's not the best way."

"Oh, yeah yeah yeah. Saved twenty-three cavalrymen in a blinding snowstorm, didn't he?" Eric winked at Jackson. "Didn't I hear you mention that once or twice? Or, like, five times maybe."

"Hey, Mr. Amusement," Nathan said, holding out the stick, "feel free. Show me what you got."

Eric waved his hand in the air. "Nah, nah, you're doing great."

Melissa arrived moments later. "We wanted to help."

Nathan looked up. "We?"

"Me and Jackson."

"He's been sitting here for five minutes and hasn't said a word to me about helping."

"Well, uh, did you ask him?" Melissa said.

Nathan scrubbed away with the stick, felt the tip. He wanted to keep going, but he felt like he'd just run out of gas. Finally he held the stick out to Jackson. "The tip's getting hot. Maybe you can put it over the top."

Jackson looked at the stick dubiously. "Yeah, maybe. But I got a better way."

"No, listen, I'm serious. You're not tired. Just do it this way and it'll work. It's gonna spark any second."

"Still . . ."

"If you start talking about the twiddle-it-between-your-palms method, I'm gonna choke you!" Nathan said with a strained smile. "No, seriously though, this is a valid approach. Let's just make it work."

Jackson looked at Melissa, then shrugged.

Then he took the stick from Nathan's outstretched hand. Nathan stood up slowly. His whole body felt sore and cramped from being hunched over in the same position for the past half hour. Jackson knelt down and started rubbing the stick.

Nathan pointed at the little pile of tinder. "Keep it close to the stick."

As Jackson began furiously rubbing the stick together, Daley ran up and said, "We need fire now!"

"Oh," Nathan said. "*Now* it's important."

"Sort of," Lex said.

He pointed to Daley's legs. Nathan's eyes widened. There must have been dozens of black worms hanging off the backs of her legs. Leeches.

"Whoa!" Eric said.

"Eeeyyyw!" Melissa squealed.

"Pardon me while I retch," Eric said.

"We can't pull 'em off," Lex said. "We need to burn them off."

Jackson looked up, still rubbing the stick back and forth. "Then let's stop fooling around with this dumb caveman approach and get serious about—"

"No!" Nathan said. "Don't stop! We're almost there!"

Jackson glared up at Nathan, then shook his head like he was disgusted about something.

"Go, Jackson!" Nathan said.

Jackson kept methodically rubbing the stick back and forth in the grooved piece of wood. He looked up at Lex. "Can those leeches do damage? I mean, serious damage?"

Lex scratched his head. "They're not poisonous or anything. Just bloodthirsty."

"Hurry, Jackson!" Daley said, shivering. "This is the only way."

Jackson looked at Daley for a while, then gave Nathan a last even stare. "Well, in that case . . ."

Jackson started rubbing furiously with the stick.

"Smoke!" Nathan said.

"Where?" Daley said.

"I don't see it, dude," Eric said.

Jackson just kept rubbing. But after a while he began to slow, and his breathing became ragged and loud.

Finally he gave it one last furious rally, then held the tip up to the tinder. Nothing. Not a puff of smoke.

"I'm done," he said, lying back.

"Eric." Nathan held up the stick.

Eric pointed at his own chest. "Who? Me?"

But then he got down on his knees and rubbed for a while. He wasn't exactly trying hard. Daley paced back and forth, arms tightly clasped around her chest, looking down sourly at him.

Nathan eventually got fed up with watching Eric's halfhearted efforts, so he grabbed the stick out of his hand and began rubbing away again. His arms felt like rubber. He couldn't maintain the rapid strokes that were necessary to really get the thing heating up. Finally he handed the stick to Lex.

Lex had a lot of energy for a kid, staring fixedly at the point of the stick. It seemed pitiful to Nathan that a ten-year-old kid could show up somebody like Eric who was, like, five years older. After a minute, a tiny bit of smoke drifted up.

The magazine! Nathan realized he had totally forgotten about the magazine. He pulled the copy of *InStyle* out from under a log, ripped several strips of paper out, and put them next to the rest of the tinder.

"Hey!" Taylor grabbed the magazine out of his hand, scattering the tinder. "What do you think you're doing?"

She stormed away in a huff.

Everybody looked at the scattered tinder, then at the point of the stick in Lex's hand. No smoke, no ember.

"Nice," Eric said.

Melissa tried. Nothing.

Jackson tried. There was a distinct smell of smoke, but nothing visible.

Nathan tried again. This time he was definitely getting smoke. "Melissa!" he said. "Tinder. Get those magazine strips right up close!"

Melissa pushed the tinder right up to the edge of the groove in the wood. Nathan felt a surge of energy. Almost!

Now smoke was coming out from under the wood in a steady stream.

"Yes!" Eric said.

"Come on! Come on!" Daley urged.

"You can do it!" Melissa said softly. "I know you can!"

Nathan rubbed harder and harder. "Almost! Almost!" he muttered. He gave the stick one last hard jab to put it over the top and . . .

The stick broke with a loud snap. The tip went spinning through the air.

Smoke streamed from the tip and Nathan could see the tiny ember tracing a red arc as it flew upward and then landed. It scattered sparks. Nathan seized a handful of paper strips, vaulted forward, pushed the strips onto the end of the stick.

But he could see it was too late. By the time he'd gotten there, the minuscule ember had gone black and dead.

Nathan slumped forward, burying his face in the ground.

He could feel the circle of eyes staring down at him. For a long time, no one spoke. The feeling of disappointment was thick in the air.

Jackson

These guys are making me crazy.

There's stuff I could be doing to help. But I don't even know if I want to. Everybody's running around trying to do things, but nobody's listening.

It's like everybody's trying to be the top dog. Well, some of us are anyway. What do we even need a top dog for? Most of the stuff we need to do is just common sense. But these guys are making it into this big power game. Who's gonna be the leader? Who's in charge? Who's gonna get the citizenship award?

Who cares?

TWELVE

A few minutes later, everyone was sitting around the fire pit, staring gloomily at the place where the fire should have been. Nathan studied it. He'd done everything right. Arranged the stone in a ring to help retain heat, lined the bottom with dry sand to keep the temperature up. He'd carefully sorted the wood by size and dryness. He'd used the best method he knew of. And he'd worked until his arms hurt.

And all for nothing. For *nothing*!

The shadows were getting long now, and the steady wind off the sea that had seemed pleasant earlier was now starting to feel a little damp and chilly. Nathan wished Captain Russell would get back. Earlier it had seemed kind of cool, getting all Swiss Family Robinson. Like a big adventure. But everything was easier in books. In books, you rubbed a couple sticks together and, presto, fire. The reality of this "adventure" was that if Captain Russell didn't find somebody to help them, they were going to spend a long time being cold, hungry, and wet. And what if somebody got sick? What if somebody broke a leg? What if ... Nathan started getting this cold feeling in his chest.

He looked around the circle. Daley kept staring at the worms on her legs. Her face was looking pale. Nathan wasn't sure if it was the blood loss or just the changing light. "They're getting bloated now," she said morosely.

"Eeyew," Taylor said.

"I am so sorry," Melissa said. "This is my fault."

Nathan shook his head. "No. No, it's not. This is on me. I thought I knew what I was doing. I really did. And I tried and ... Well, anyway that's beside the point. What I'm saying is, I took my frustration out on you, Mel. And that's not right. I'm sorry."

Melissa smiled her bright smile at Nathan. It made him feel a little better. A little, but not a lot.

"Yeah, okay," Daley said. "I mean, that's sweet and all. But I'm still getting my blood sucked."

"Once again, eeyeew!" Taylor said.

"So what do we do?" Eric said. "Daley's gonna need a transfusion pretty soon. And it's getting dark."

"Where do you think Captain Russell is?" Melissa said.

Nobody answered.

The shadows in the forest around them that had looked cool and inviting just a few minutes ago were now beginning to take on a forbidding look. Nathan tried to shake the cold feeling in his chest. But it just seemed to keep getting stronger and stronger.

The only sounds were the waves and the wind. Melissa hugged her knees tightly to her chest. Daley shivered.

Finally Jackson stood up. He looked calmly around the ring of kids. As always, there was something slightly menacing in his eyes. And something disapproving, too.

"Well?" he said, his gaze stopping for a minute on Daley's

face, then on Nathan's. "You two ready to listen to somebody else now?"

"What do you mean?" Daley said.

Nathan shrugged. "Listen to who?"

"Me, just for instance."

"Sure," Nathan said. "I'm out of ideas."

"And I suppose you have one. . . ." Daley said. She didn't sound challenging, just worn-out and defeated.

Jackson reached into his pocket, came out with a small gleaming object. Then he picked up Taylor's magazine and tore off the cover.

Taylor didn't say anything.

Jackson flicked the object in his hand. It was a lighter. A tiny flame wavered and flickered in the breeze. He held it up to the cover of the magazine.

On the cover, the beautiful woman in the bathing suit turned dark, wrinkled up, and began to burn. In seconds she was gone. Jackson tossed the burning cover onto Nathan's neat pile of tinder.

Everyone stared, unbelieving.

"You gotta look around, man," Jackson said. "We're all dancing at the same party."

The tinder sputtered, then flamed up. The fire came to life.

THIRTEEN

Melissa watched the fire leap and hiss. Nathan had made a teepee of sticks and they were blazing away. Why had Jackson taken so long to let everybody know he had a lighter? She couldn't figure the guy out.

Apparently she wasn't the only one who wondered. Nathan leaned over and said, "Hey, Jackson, not that I'm mad or anything . . . But couldn't you have dragged out that lighter a couple minutes earlier?"

Jackson shrugged.

"Were you trying to teach me some kind of lesson?" Nathan said.

Jackson didn't answer.

"Maybe," Daley said, "it's because every time he suggested there might be a flaw in your brilliant idea, you wouldn't listen."

Nathan rolled his eyes.

"Maybe he just forgot he had it," Taylor said. "People forget stuff sometimes."

"Maybe he just likes cultivating that man-of-mystery thing," Eric said.

"Or maybe—" Melissa started to defend him, but before she had a chance, Jackson stood up slowly and walked away from the fire.

"Oops!" Nathan said. "I think we offended the man of mystery."

"Come on, guys," Melissa said. "Don't you think you're being a little mean?"

"Hey, he's the one who sat there for an hour like some wooden statue while I wore my arms out," Nathan said.

"And while my legs were covered with leeches," Daley added.

"Well, it just seems like it wouldn't hurt to thank him," Melissa said. "If it weren't for him, we'd be sitting around freezing our butts off while the sun goes down."

Melissa noticed Jackson grab the video camera off a box next to the plane. Then he disappeared into the darkness.

"Hey, we didn't mean anything by it, Jackson!" Eric called. "We think that you're a very beautiful and special person, and we all love you very deeply."

Melissa threw a tiny piece of kindling at him.

"Ow!" Eric said. "You could have put my eye out."

Jackson

Life's strange.

I read that book *Robinson Crusoe* when I was in seventh grade. For two years I had this whole thing going on in my head, like I was Robinson Crusoe. I'd sit around my house drawing pictures and imagining things. How to make a house out of palm fronds.

How to hunt for wild pigs. How to make a bow and arrow. You name it. I guess I just wanted to be by myself. I wanted to be out there where it was all up to me, where nobody else could drag me down.

The school I went to back then was in this crap neighborhood and had a lot of gang stuff happening, and here I am, this quiet white kid who likes to read. Not so fun.

So I had to find somebody to hang with—or eventually I was gonna get seriously busted up. So that's what I did. You do what you gotta do. Once I started hanging with the right kind of guys, tough kids—nah, nobody bothered me anymore. And I stopped thinking about being Robinson Crusoe.

But then, at a certain point, rolling with people who can protect you—that starts causing its own little problems. Problems that could land you in juvie if you weren't careful.

So to get out of that life, I had to do some other stuff. Which resulted in my ending up at the Hartwell School. It was like being back in seventh grade in a way. Being the odd guy out all the time. But—tell you the truth? That's how I want it. I still want to be Robinson Crusoe. Out there, all alone, nobody else to drag you down. You rise or fall on your own efforts.

Funny. Here I am, doing it up like Robinson Crusoe.

Only problem—once again—everybody else is cramping my style. Once again, it's me and a bunch of . . . No, let's put it this way—these kids, if they think, they don't listen. Or if they listen, they don't think. Same story, different town.

I'm not interested in getting caught up in their little power plays. If they want to get all bent out of shape about who's telling who to do what—hey, fine. But not me. If they want to listen to me when I've got something to contribute, fine. They don't, that's cool, too.

So why am I laughing? Because everybody else is freaking out. Me? Nah. Truth? I'm happy to be here.

Anywhere is better than where I'm from.

Daley lay on her stomach in the sand. Lex had a stick with an ember on the end. He was methodically touching the ember to the leeches. At first Daley had been convinced he was going to burn her. But he had the patience and focus of a surgeon. Boy, she had to give her little brother credit. He was a pretty cool kid.

"Last one," Lex said.

"Careful," Daley said.

The leech shriveled up and fell off.

"This is *so* gross," Taylor said.

Daley stood up, turned to look at the sunset. Nathan stood next to her, looking out at the bloodred sun sinking into the sea. The wind had started feeling pretty chilly coming off the sea. It felt good to have the fire. And not just because it had gotten rid of her leeches.

"Guess we better think about setting up camp," Nathan said. "You find a good spot?"

"Sure," Daley said. "If you don't mind sleeping on top of a colony of blood-sucking vampire leeches."

"Well, at least the weather should be good," Eric said. "What is it—red sky at night, sailors delight?"

"No," Lex said. "Actually that's an old wives' tale. Frequently a red sky at night means there's a lot of humidity in the air. Humidity that could precede significant precipitation."

"Where did you get this kid?" Eric said to Daley. "Is he, like, a Klingon or something?"

"You mean Vulcan," Lex said. "Vulcans are the brainy ones. Klingons are the fighters."

"Lex's point," Daley snapped at Eric, "is that we need to make camp. Now."

"Thank you for that clarification," Eric said. "Actually, thank you both. Because that Vulcan-Klingon thing has been bugging me for a long, long ..." Eric's voice trailed off under Daley's withering gaze.

FOURTEEN

The crack of thunder woke Daley with a start. She sat up and looked around the dark tent. A light came on, illuminating Taylor and Melissa. Outside the tent Daley could see palm trees thrashing wildly against the driving rain. A hard wind hammered at the tent. Thank goodness she'd had the foresight to make them bring all their gear in the tents. Otherwise all their stuff would be getting soaked by now.

She just hoped that the tent could take this kind of wind without blowing away. So far it felt reasonably sturdy.

Daley looked over at Taylor, who was clutching a flashlight.

"I wouldn't hold that," Daley said.

"Why not?"

"It's metal. There's lightning. You could get electrocuted."

Taylor stared at her for a moment, then thrust the flashlight into Melissa's hand. Melissa tossed it into the corner of the tent.

In the boys' tent a battery-powered camp light was already lit. There was even more gear in their tent than in the girls' tent. And there were more boys. It was way too crowded.

Lex opened the zipper and looked out. The rain was driving sideways in the wind and the black trees writhed and twisted against the sky. The thunder was nearly continuous, and streaks of light raced across the sky. "The lightning is spectacular!" he said.

"Yeah, great. Why don't you go out in it?" Eric said. "Then maybe I'll have room to sleep."

"Speaking of which," Jackson said, "is that your hand on my—"

"Dude, no!" Eric snatched his hand away.

Nathan ran his hand along the bottom of the tent. "Water's building up out there. Daley sure picked a fabulous spot to camp."

Back in the girls' tent Daley said, "Sure is great that Nathan spent so much time on that fire. Lotta good it's doing us."

"It got your leeches off."

"Yeah—after Jackson took over and started it."

Eric tried to sit up. He banged his head on the lamp hanging above his bed.

"Ow! There's no room in here."

"Thank Daley for that," Nathan said. "If she'd had any sense, we'd have left all this junk in the plane to begin with. But no, she's worried some tsunami's gonna come and wash away the plane."

Jackson banged Eric in the ribs with his elbow.

"Hey!" Eric said.

"Like there's gonna be a tsunami *today*," Nathan said bitterly.

Eric jerked on his sleeping bag, trying to get it away from Jackson. Water had begun to leak into the tent. "Dude, give me some room," Eric said.

Jackson only burrowed deeper into his sleeping bag.

"Thanks, Daley," Eric said. "This is really great."

Thunder crashed. Outside, a tree fell in the driving wind, smashing into the wet ground with a loud smack. In the girls' tent, Mel and Taylor screamed.

"Don't do that!" Daley said. "If we show weakness, Nathan will walk all over us."

"Guys," Nathan said. "Stop complaining. If we show weakness, Daley will walk all over us."

"He's on some kind of power trip," Daley said.

"Give her an inch and she'll take a mile," Nathan said.

"He's totally over his head. He thinks because he's an Eagle Scout and he's read a couple of musty old books about explorers that he's some kind of expert!"

"She doesn't listen . . ."

"... he's arrogant ..."

"... she's an ego case ..."

"... he's a poseur ..."

"... she's power-hungry ..."

"... conceited, selfish, boring ..."

"... stubborn, self-centered, bossy, bad breath."

Jackson sat up suddenly, his face hard. "That's it! I've had enough!"

Nathan stared at him for a minute. "What?"

FIFTEEN

Melissa

I am so frustrated! Every time I turn around, Daley and Nathan are ragging on each other. It's making me crazy.

Am I just being a wimp? I mean, I'm Nathan's best friend. So I guess I should take his side. Shouldn't I? But every time it starts, I get this twisted-up feeling in my stomach and I just want to run off and hide in the jungle. Plus, if I thought they were ever gonna resolve anything, I suppose I could just be like, *Hey, I'll just stick my fingers in my ears and let you two go ahead and fight it out.* But I don't see any end in sight. All this competition just seems to be splitting us apart. And right now, that's just not a good thing.

First, Captain Russell goes wandering off into the jungle and doesn't come back. What's next? Nathan and Daley splitting apart and each taking half the group with them? Pretty soon it'll be everybody for

themselves. I mean, I guess Captain Russell will get
back and pull everything together soon. But what
if he doesn't? We really need to get this settled.
Soon!

I have an idea. I'm gonna talk to the others and see
what they think . . .

"I said, *enough!*" Jackson said.

It was morning. The storm was gone. The beach was once
again a beautiful strip of white, and the sky was a cloudless
blue. Paradise had returned.

Once again, Nathan and Daley were glaring at each other,
getting into it over some little thing. After a moment, they
both looked away sheepishly. Nathan's shirt was on inside
out and Daley's hair was sticking up. Everybody looked
hollow-eyed and exhausted after their sleepless night.

"God, you sound like my parents," Eric said.

"Really," Taylor said. "Yip yip yip yip yip." She held up
her hands like little puppets, mouths open, bickering with
each other.

"I'm just trying to do what's best," Daley said sullenly.

"Yeah," Nathan said. "Like you'd even know what that
was."

"Hey, show us how it's done. Get out your grandpa's little
book and demonstrate your brilliant woodcraft, O Master
Firemaker."

"*Great-great* grandfather."

"Yeah, whatever."

"*Stop!*" Jackson said. His voice wasn't loud, but somehow
it startled everybody into silence.

"Guys, we've been talking . . ." Melissa said.

"Who has?" Daley demanded.

"Everybody," Melissa said.

"Everybody but you two," Eric added.

"We agree that it's probably good for somebody to take charge. But since you guys can't agree on who it should be ..."

"... we thought a friendly little competition would settle things," Eric said.

"What kind of competition?" Nathan said.

"You have all morning to prove to us who's the better leader."

"Then we'll vote," Lex added.

"Unless we get rescued, of course," Taylor added brightly.

"So ... it's like a campaign," Nathan said.

"Yeah," Eric said. "A campaign to keep you two from driving us crazy."

Melissa looked at them each in turn. "Okay. You up for it?"

Nathan looked at Daley. Daley looked at Nathan. After they eyed each other for a moment, Nathan stuck out his hand. Daley grabbed it and they shook.

"May the best man win," Nathan said.

"You mean the best woman?" Daley said.

"Yeah, right," Nathan said.

"You're toast."

SIXTEEN

"I'll tell you her problem," Nathan said. He and Melissa were stretching the tent out, hanging it over a line to dry.

"I can't wait to hear," Melissa said. She was Nathan's best friend, but, *man* . . . She was feeling like she wouldn't mind a little space right now. Ever since he lost the election back in school, it was like he was obsessing about Daley. He had always been a competitive guy—but this was ridiculous.

Nathan waved his finger in the air. "Leadership is about delegation. She doesn't understand that. She's a micromanager. You know? She's got to do every freakin' little thing herself."

Melissa didn't say anything. She pulled the tent over the line and started straightening it.

"Here, let me do that," Nathan said. "You want to get the maximum amount of it facing the sun. See?"

Melissa held her hands up like *I surrender* and stepped back. "Delegation. Right."

"Can you and Jackson get the fire started again?"

"Sure."

"Cool." Nathan looked over Melissa's shoulder like he was looking for something. "So . . . uh . . . you know what Daley's gonna do?"

"I think she's working out a schedule to ration the food and . . ."

"Oh! Yes! Isn't that just too perfect? Control, control, control."

Melissa stood with her arms folded across her chest while Nathan fussed with the tent.

"See, Mel, what I'm gonna do is go out in the jungle and find food. This is a tropical jungle. I'm sure there's food out there practically dripping off the trees. Bananas, coconuts, screw pine, berries. I'm gonna come back with a load of grub and it's gonna make her whole plan into a total joke."

"Why don't you take somebody with you?"

"Wanna come?"

"Uh . . ." Melissa wasn't sure how much more of his complaining about Daley she could take. "Why don't you go with Eric?"

"That guy's useless. I'll just go by myself."

"Maybe you shouldn't go by yourself."

"Nah, I won't go far. Besides, the main thing here is I need to prove what I can do. It would sort of water down the impact if somebody else helped me."

He gave one last tug on the tent, then trotted off into the jungle. As soon as he disappeared, the tent began sliding slowly off the line. Within seconds it was a wet heap of nylon on the ground.

Melissa sighed. "Bye, Mr. Delegation," she said, waving at the jungle. "See ya. Thanks. Bye. Keep up the good work."

Nathan

I know there's been tension. That's natural. We've got a lot of stuff to worry about. The food situation. The water. The camp location. The fire.

But I'm gonna get it all straightened out. They'll see.

So right now I figure Daley's got Lex's vote for sure. He's her little brother, that's cool, I'm not gonna even bother trying to get his vote.

Melissa's a lock for me. I got her working on Jackson. She'll tell him all about why he ought to vote for me. So all I have to do is win over Eric and Taylor. And Taylor pretty much can't stand Daley because Daley's always telling her to do stuff she doesn't want to do ... so ...

... V for Victory, baby.

Lex dropped the plastic bin full of gear on the ground near the plane, then sat on top of it and took a couple of deep breaths. Man! This junk was *heavy*. Daley, meanwhile, was carrying her clipboard, checking things off and making notes in her neat, tiny handwriting.

"Please, don't make me move this stuff again," Lex said.

"Last stop. We'll store it on the plane from now on."

Lex sighed. "Like I said yesterday ..." he murmured.

"Excuse me?" Daley said.

"Nothing, nothing, nothing."

Daley continued her inventory, her brow furrowing as she worked.

"What's the matter, Daley?"

Daley scratched through something, then added up some figures. Finally she looked up at Lex and said, "This is not good. We don't have as much food and water as I thought. When I tell everybody, they're gonna blame me."

"Why? It's not your fault."

"No, but if I ration it, I'll be the bad guy and then nobody will vote for me."

"Well, you can't lie."

Daley hesitated. "No." The corner of her mouth turned up slightly. "But I could, ah, fudge it a little." She looked at Lex and the smile went away. "Just until the election."

"That's not fair."

"Fair? This isn't about *fair*. This is politics." She pointed her pencil at the plane. "Check the plane for any food or water we might have missed."

Lex frowned, then stood and walked toward the plane shaking his head. Sometimes it seemed like life had been a lot better back before he had a big sister.

Jackson and Melissa walked up to the fire ring and surveyed the area. The wood that was left was all completely soaked. Jackson picked up a piece of driftwood, squeezed it with his hand. The wet wood crumbled under his fingers.

He scowled, threw the wood back on the sand.

Melissa picked through the pile of remaining wood, finally looked up and said, "No way any of this stuff is going to burn."

"Put it in the sun," Jackson said.

They began moving the wood out farther onto the beach.

"Maybe we should stack it loosely so the wind will flow through and help dry it out," Melissa said.

Jackson nodded. "Good thinking."

Melissa felt a surge of pleasure. How long since Nathan had said anything like that to her? Not since they'd been on the island, that's for sure.

"So?" Melissa said. "Who you gonna vote for?"

"Vote?" Jackson raised one eyebrow. "What for?"

"Well, I mean, we do need a leader. At least until Captain Russell gets back."

Jackson tossed a few more pieces of wood on the pile, then shrugged dismissively. "Hardly matters," he said. "They're both nuts."

Melissa laughed. "I've known them both for a long time. They're good guys. They're just scared, like all of us. And so they're trying too hard."

Jackson finished stacking the wood, then stood up and brushed off his hands. Melissa noticed that his hands were callused, like he did hard physical work. She wondered what he did to make his hands look like that. They were nice hands, though. Strong hands.

"I saw a big pile of driftwood down there." Jackson pointed down the beach. "Think I'll wander on over there and see if any of it's worth keeping."

Melissa waited for him to invite her to come with him, but he didn't. He just walked away without looking back.

"Okay," she called. "I'll, uh . . . I'll go check in the jungle, see if I can find any dead wood lying around."

Jackson put his earphones on and kept walking.

Melissa

I don't know if this election was such a brilliant idea. I almost hate to admit this, but Nathan's been driving me bananas with all this competitive stuff.

And Daley? God, she's totally off the charts. I mean, they're both nice people and everything, but ...

It's like the election is doing the opposite of what it was supposed to do. I mean what if instead of everybody getting behind one leader, this vote splits us apart? What if we'd have two groups who don't agree instead of only two people? That would be a real mess. Maybe I made a big mistake suggesting this election.

I just keep feeling like there's something I could be doing better, something that would make the whole situation calm down. But it seems like everything I do just makes matters worse.

Oops. Gotta—

Hearing footsteps behind her, Melissa quickly turned off the video camera. She tried to hide the camera as she turned around. It was Taylor.

"Whatcha doing?" Taylor said.

"Nothing!" Melissa said.

Taylor gave her a skeptical look. "Please don't say that, Melissa. Because that would mean you were talking to yourself. Which, frankly, would be very disturbing."

"Alright. I'm just ... making a video diary."

Taylor reached around Melissa's back, grabbed the camera. She examined it, a sly expression forming on her face.

"You mean like telling your side of what's happening?" Taylor said.

"Exactly. For after we get rescued. Nathan's doing one, too. We each have our own tape. That way we can keep them separate." She snatched the camera back, popped out the cassette. "And private."

Taylor rolled her eyes. "God. Don't get all twitchy. I don't want to see your dumb video." She thought about something for a minute, then smiled. "You know, I might want to make one, too, though."

"I don't know ..." Melissa said. She didn't like the idea of the camera becoming communal property. Plus, Taylor was not exactly the most responsible person.

"Hey!" Taylor said, acting all hurt. "I'm stuck here just like you."

Melissa thought about it. If she didn't do what Taylor wanted, Taylor would be bugging her and complaining at every opportunity. She'd probably end up taking the camera anyway. No, better to just let her have it and make sure she knew how to use it so she wouldn't mess it up.

Melissa stuffed her own tape into the pocket of her pants, then handed the camera to Taylor. "The tapes are in the plane. But be quick when you're shooting because when the battery runs down, that's it. It's over."

"Really?" Taylor looked all huggy-kissy, now that she'd gotten her way. "I thought it's over when you let go of the little red button."

Melissa looked at her for a minute. Was she really serious? Or was this just some kind of act?

"Just don't waste the battery," Melissa said. "Okay?"

Taylor gave her a quick hug. "You rock, Mel!"

Then she hustled off back toward the beach.

"Don't waste the—"

And then Taylor was gone.

Nathan had figured that finding food wouldn't be that big a deal. Tropical jungles were supposed to be stuffed with fruits. He'd studied up on the natural food sources in Micronesia. There were bananas, mangos, star fruit, papayas, coconuts. Plus all these weird fruits you didn't see in the States—like rambutan and durian and screw pine . . . Plus all kinds of berries and nuts and roots. It should have been easy. Unfortunately he'd been searching for half an hour and there was no sign of any of those things.

Well, except for coconuts.

There were a bazillion coconuts on the island. Problem was, they were all way up in these humongous palm trees. He'd found a couple of coconuts on the ground, cracked them open with rocks, and found them to be rotten.

So if he was going to score with the big haul of food, he was going to have to get up in one of those trees.

He stopped in front of a palm tree and looked up. Boy, no joke—it really was pretty tall. But there were two nice big clumps of coconuts. Enough food for a couple of meals right there. Coconut milk was very high in vitamins and calories. At home everybody freaked out about calories. But here you needed them. Calories were what kept you going. Calories were energy. And energy was life.

Maybe there was a way to get at the coconuts besides climbing. He picked up a fallen palm frond, stripped off most of the leafy part, leaving the woody core, then heaved it up at the tree. The frond twisted and whirled in the air. It missed. He tried again. It missed again. The thing was impossible to aim.

He looked around for something more predictable. After hunting around for ten minutes, he found a rock the size of his fist. He heaved it up at the coconuts. It hit smack in the middle of the coconuts with a satisfying thud.

The coconuts didn't move.

He tried again. This time, he missed. The rock went flying into the jungle.

"Aw man!" There was no way he'd find the rock again.

He looked up at the tree. He'd have to climb. Well, so be it. How hard could it be, right?

He grabbed hold of the trunk with his hands, then began to climb. Or—he tried to anyway. His shoes got no traction and slipped right off the surface of the tree. Apparently the tree had been perfectly engineered to make it hard to climb. Just rough enough to make it rip up his hands, just smooth enough to give no traction for his shoes. He took off his shoes, tried climbing barefoot. He got about three feet off the ground, fell off. A palm frond on the ground stabbed him in the arch of his foot.

"Ouch! Ow! God!"

When he finally determined that there was no bleeding, he put his shoes back on. He looked up at the tree. There had to be a way. If Micronesian tribespeople who didn't even know what a wheel was could get coconuts down from a palm tree—so could he.

The question was—how?

He kicked the tree. Which only succeeded in hurting his foot. Now he was starting to get mad. He paced around, threw a couple more branches up in the air. No luck.

He stared up at the tree some more. It reminded him of a telephone pole. How did they climb telephone poles, anyway? Suddenly it struck him!

"Yes!" he said.

He began taking off his shirt.

Lex was searching through the stuff from the luggage compartment in the belly of the plane. Sure, Daley had been through it already. But Daley was—well, she had her own way of seeing things. And if something didn't match her little preconceived idea about what was important, then she just didn't see it at all.

He had found a treasure trove of electronic goodies in a box. Based on the name and address listed on the label on the side of the box, it appeared that they were being sent to somebody in Palau who had nothing to do with the camping trip.

He looked inside, found four or five circuit boards, all of them packed in bubble wrap. He pulled one out and looked at it. It didn't mean anything to him. Just a bunch of resistors and chips and capacitors and stuff.

He unpacked the next and the next and the next. All of them were inscrutable. And probably totally useless. He was considering quitting. There was only one more piece of electronics in the box—the largest piece. Well, he might as well open it, right? Worst-case scenario he could use it as a surfboard or something.

He ripped off the bubble wrap. His eyes widened.

"Oh, excellent!" he said.

"What?" Daley said. "Did you find some food?"

Daley was looking over his shoulder.

"Oh," she said, disappointed. "Great."

"No, this is really excellent. It's—"

"Please, Lex." She held up one hand. "Don't go off on some tangent about how this is going to speed up your video-game graphics or something. If it's not food, I don't want to hear about it."

"Yeah, but this is so cool—"

"Whoa, hup, nope!" She waved her hands in front of it. "I have an election to win. If it's not food, it's not helping."

She turned and walked away.

"But . . ." Lex watched her walk away, then frowned. Maybe someday she'd learn to listen. Wouldn't that be a nice change?

He rewrapped the electronic panel in the bubble wrap. Better be careful. This thing was going to be really valuable.

Then he stuck it back in the box, and put the box back in the storage compartment.

Taylor

I'm standing with my feet in warm South Pacific water on an unknown island. Is it a tropical paradise? Or hell on earth?

Hello, I'm Taylor Hagan, and you're watching my story.

So far our luck has been good. When the lame pilot of our mangled plane panicked in the middle of a typhoon, I seized the controls and landed us safely on the stretch of magnificent beach you see behind me.

Now it's up to me to keep this ragtag band of castaways alive. Food, water, shelter—the challenges are coming thick and fast. And you'll follow my story as it happens.

Totally live. Totally real.

Join me, won't you?

Eric adjusted the camera. "Okay, hold on, Taylor, hold on. I need to get the thingamajig . . ." He wasn't quite sure about the controls. How did you zoom out? Oh, there it was. He thumbed the silver button again.

"Okay, Taylor, now walk!"

Taylor was wearing her bathing suit with a little scarf thingy thrown around her hips. Her hair and the scarf blew in the breeze. Back in Hollywood, they had ten-thousand-dollar wind machines just to make models look this natural. And this hot! Taylor flipped her hair, then lowered her eyelashes and looked at the camera as she walked along the shore.

"Yeah, yeah!" Eric called, waving his hand in a circle, showing her to keep it up. "Work it. Work it. This is B.O., baby. You are totally B.O."

Taylor stopped and made a wincing, irritated face. "B.O.? Excuse me?"

"Not like 'body odor.'"

"You said B.O."

"Right. B.O. 'Box Office.' B.O. is showbiz for 'Box Office.'"

"B.O."

"You're money, baby. Totally Box Office. When they see this tape, the Hollywood guys are gonna be fighting each other to make your movie. We're gonna make you famous."

"And rich?" Taylor cocked her head flirtatiously.

"Same thing."

"Awesome!"

Eric pointed at the plane. "Now let's shoot the scene where you single-handedly save the plane from being washed out to sea."

"But isn't that, like—fake?"

Eric took an establishing shot of the tail section of the plane with the numbers 29 DWN on it, then panned across the long white beach over to where Taylor was standing. Very artsy, the way he shot it.

"I mean, shouldn't I use both hands?" Taylor said.

Eric blinked. He considered explaining what single-handed meant. Nah, what was the use?

He checked the little battery icon on the camera. No problem. Plenty of juice left.

"Let's get you over by the plane," he said.

She held up her hands to her hair. "Do I need to comb it again?" she said. "I don't want to look all gross and scruffy while I'm pulling the plane out of the water."

"Good thinking," Eric said. "You definitely don't want that."

They started walking toward the plane.

Nathan took off his flannel shirt, twirled it around until it was bunched up like a rope. Then he studied the palm tree.

Okay. So the trick was going to be coming up the side of the palm tree that was a little bit bent over. He'd have better traction that way. He squinted. This side. Yes.

He looped one end of the shirt around the tree. It was thinking about telephone poles that had given him the solution. Telephone linemen climbed poles by hooking a long leather belt around the pole, then sort of walking up the pole while the belt supported their weight. Of course it kinda helped that they had six-inch-long steel spikes on their shoes.

But the principle was still there. Hold your weight with the shirt, lean back, walk the feet up the tree. Then move the shirt. Repeat until you get to the top. Then snag a big honking pile of coconuts.

He tied the sleeves of the shirt around his waist, put his feet on the trunk about six inches off the ground, then leaned back, supporting his weight on the tree.

Hey! It worked.

He inched the shirt up. Without spikes on his feet, he sort of had to grip the tree. But it did work.

He moved his feet, inched up again.

Feet, shirt.

Feet, shirt.

It was hard work. But each time you got the shirt repositioned, you could rest your feet so you didn't get worn out.

"I am a genius!" Nathan muttered. "Once everybody sees this, Daley will be lucky to get *any* votes."

He looked down. Three feet. He looked up. About thirty feet to go. Whew. This was a lot of work.

He braced his feet and began moving the shirt again.

When he'd shifted the shirt, he noticed something moving on the tree. Ants? Some kind of little bugs. Lots of them. He tried to sweep them away with his hands, but taking his hands off the tree made the shirt stretch. He was afraid if he put too much weight on the shirt, one of the arms might rip off.

Well, what was the big deal about a few dinky bugs? Bugs were nothing.

He repositioned the shirt again. Then his feet. Then the shirt again.

He looked down again. Four feet.

Feet. Shirt.

Feet. Shirt.

When he saw the thing moving on the tree, he thought it was just one of the harmless-looking little bugs.

But then he realized it wasn't. It was a spider. A huge, hairy, freaky-looking spider. The biggest spider Nathan had ever seen. It was moving slowly down the tree toward his hand.

Nathan was not the world's biggest fan of spiders. He reached out and tried to flick the huge spider away, but it was out of reach.

He tried to move his feet so he could reposition the shirt. But his legs suddenly felt like they were made from blocks of ice.

"Come on, bro," he said to himself. "It's just a tiny bug."

Then the spider got to his hand. He couldn't let go of the tree yet, though, or the shirt would rip. He felt the hairy little legs hit his knuckles.

Oh no. This is not happening, he thought. *This is not—*

Eric and Taylor reviewed the tape in the cabin of the plane. Taylor was pulling on the rope, her hips dashed with sea foam, her long, neatly combed hair blowing picturesquely in the breeze.

"I needed my line!" Taylor said irritably. "You forgot to give me my line."

"Doesn't matter."

"'It's moving now!' I was supposed to yell, 'The plane's moving now!' You forgot to give me my line."

"That's what I'm saying," Eric said. "It doesn't matter. You could be saying anything. Because you look great."

"Really?"

"Taylor, trust me. I know these things. My dad's in the business. Comedy's about the lines. Not drama. Drama's all about the visual. You can say any old crap as long as you look good."

"You're sure?"

"Totally. See how fabulous you look." He froze the frame. The wind was catching her hair and the muscles in her arms were straining. Her skin glistened in the sun.

Taylor studied the picture. "You're right," she said finally. "I look fabulous." She gave him a coy smile. "I've got B.O., baby."

"B.O.!"

She grabbed his arm. "Let's go celebrate!"

Taylor pulled him by the arm out the door. He felt a warm glow of satisfaction. She was digging him, man. Totally digging him.

A momentary thought flashed through his mind. Had he turned the camera off?

And then Taylor rubbed her shoulder against his arm and flipped her blond hair and laughed. And Eric forgot about everything else but Taylor.

Nathan watched the spider walk onto his hand. Would it bite him? Right now he couldn't take his hands off the tree or he'd fall.

He felt paralyzed, numb. If it walked onto him, it could walk off. Right? *Get off me!* he wanted to scream. Like that would do any good. . . . The second he let out a peep was the second Daley would show up and make him look like a fool.

The huge spider's feet waved in the air for a moment. It seemed in no rush to do anything. After a moment's consideration, it began to slowly walk up his arm.

"Hey, guys!" Daley said as Eric and Taylor walked out of the plane. "I've been looking for you. You need some water?"

"What happened to the whole rationing thing?" Eric said.

Lex, who was standing nearby, had been about to ask her the same question.

"Not your problem," Daley said, holding out two full bottles of water. "I'll work it out. That is, if you vote for me."

Eric turned to Taylor and gave her a look of bogus astonishment. "I'm shocked. That is totally unethical!" He snatched the bottles from her hand. "I love it, Daley!"

He tossed one of the bottles to Taylor, who popped the top off and threw it on the sand. Then she threw her head back and squirted it into her mouth.

Eric started running toward the tree line. "Race you!" he said.

Taylor began running after him, laughing brightly. Her water bottle squirted and dribbled, spraying beads of water out into the sand, where it disappeared immediately.

Lex looked at Daley and said, "You're bribing them. With *our* water."

Daley gave him a superior look. "Hey, I'm the best person to lead this group. That's obvious to anybody. So anything I do to get elected is okay."

"How convenient," Lex said.

Daley pointed her finger at him. "I'm serious. In the long run, we'll be better off with me in charge. So what's one bottle of water in the grand scheme of things?"

"Two."

"One, two—whatever." She began walking toward the plane. "Okay, I think we're in good shape."

"We?" Lex said.

"Yeah, those two are the last two pieces in the puzzle."

"How do you figure that?"

"Well, you're going to vote for me. I get a vote. Add Taylor and Eric, that's four. Four votes to three, I win. Game over."

"And that's when you tell everybody the truth about the food and water?"

Daley smiled blandly at him. "Exactly."

"Well, before you start writing your acceptance speech, I want to show you something I found." He headed toward the storage compartment in the plane.

"Unless it's more food, it can wait."

"It's not food."

"Then it can wait."

She walked off, leaving Lex standing there in the hot sand. Lex frowned.

The spider had reached Nathan's elbow.

Okay, this was getting too close to home. He imagined it crawling up his arm, across his face. No. That wasn't working.

Even though his position was precarious, he knew he

couldn't stand having the spider on his face. That was out.

So he let go of the tree, smacked the spider. It flew through the air, landed with a loud thump in the litter of palm fronds on the ground. Unharmed, it skittered off and disappeared.

Nathan expected that the shirt would rip and he would plunge back down the tree. But amazingly, nothing happened.

Nathan felt his pulse return to normal, and a sense of well-being surged through him. He leaned back, held out his arms. He looked up at the coconuts, feeling the tree sway gently in the breeze. Hey, they didn't even seem that far away. He stretched his arms out as far as they would go, enjoying the feeling. Almost like flying.

It was like, *Look, Ma! No hands!*

Which is when his foot slipped.

Oops!

Nathan began to fall. There was a moment where he felt like he was floating in midair.

Then the shock of impact.

Everything went black.

SEVENTEEN

Lex was breaking driftwood and branches in half, handing them to Jackson, who was arranging them in the bottom of the fire pit.

"It's so cool!" Lex said. "I can't believe they had one on the plane."

"It works?"

"Absolutely. All you need is sunlight, and that's something we have plenty of."

"Did you show Daley?"

"Well, I tried to." Lex made a face. "She's too . . . she's thinking about other things. Are you gonna vote for her?"

Jackson frowned. For a minute Lex thought he was thinking about whether or not he was going to vote for Daley. But then he noticed Jackson was peering at the trees.

"What's the matter?" Lex said.

"Where's Nathan?"

Lex looked around. Daley was at the plane. Melissa was helping her. Taylor and Eric were lying on beach towels in the sand. Where *was* Nathan?

"How long has he been gone?" Lex said.

Jackson didn't answer. He just stood up and started walking toward the trees.

Melissa walked into the plane, looking for a cooking pot in case Nathan came back with some food. She was getting a little hungry. Every time she noticed the box full of dried food, her mouth started watering.

What would Nathan find? Fruit, probably. Anything else? He'd told her about all these fruits and things he'd read about—some of which sounded appetizing and some of which sounded pretty awful. She didn't care how hungry she got, she was not eating bugs or larvae or worms or any of that kind of junk. You had to draw the line somewhere, right?

Maybe Captain Russell would come back with food. For about the hundredth time, she looked out at the tree line, hoping to see the pilot's pineapple-covered Hawaiian shirt emerging from the jungle. But there was no one there, no movement, nothing but jungle and more jungle. She shivered, then forced herself to look away. When she thought too long about what was going on with Captain Russell and the others, it made her nervous.

She started thinking about food again. Maybe if she just had a taste . . .

As she was eyeing the bags of dried food that Daley had stored on the plane, she noticed the video camera sitting on a seat. Taylor and Eric were so careless! She picked it up, checked to make sure that—

"Noooooooo!" she yelled.

They had left the camera on. And now the battery had run out. Taylor was so inconsiderate!

Melissa stormed out of the plane and onto the beach,

where she found Eric and Taylor lying in the sun. Both of them appeared to be half asleep, with self-satisfied little smiles on their faces.

"Hey!" she yelled.

"Huh?" Eric said.

"You're kicking up sand!" Taylor said. "Could you do that somewhere else?"

"I told you to be careful!" Melissa said.

"Careful about what!"

"The camera! The battery's dead."

"What!" Taylor's mouth opened. "That camera's gonna be my big break. How could you let this happen, Melissa!"

"Me?" Melissa felt her face getting hot. "*You're* the one who did it."

"No, I didn't!"

"Well, it was full when I gave it to you!" Melissa said.

"Then why is it dead?"

"Aggghh!" Melissa grabbed her own hair and pulled on it. "Taylor, you are unbelievable."

"Am I unbelievable?" Taylor said to Eric.

"Yeah, but in a good way."

Melissa took Taylor's tape out of the camera and threw it on the sand. "Serves you right if you never get your stupid 'big break.'"

Melissa stormed away toward the jungle.

"What is her *problem*?" she heard Taylor saying as she walked away.

Lex and Jackson had been searching for fifteen or twenty minutes. But so far, no Nathan.

"This place makes me nervous," Lex said.

They had reached a place where gnarled old trees rose high above them, blotting out the sky. Vines as thick as Lex's legs wrapped themselves around their trunks like huge snakes. In fact Lex kept thinking that he was seeing giant pythons. Then he'd whip around and it would just be a vine.

"They don't have snakes here, you know," Lex said—more for his own reassurance than for Jackson's.

Jackson gave him a sidelong look.

"Nathan! Nathan!" Lex called. There was no answer. "Why would he go off on his own?"

Jackson shrugged, gave him a look that said, *You're asking the wrong guy.*

"He couldn't have come this far," Lex said. "I mean . . . could he?"

Jackson stood with his hands on his hips, staring into the green-tinged darkness.

Daley walked out of the trees carrying more gear from the campsite to store in the plane.

"I am so mad!" Melissa said.

"Why?" Daley said.

"I've been making a video diary. Nathan has, too. But Taylor borrowed the camera and ran the battery down."

"Oh yeah?"

"God! Why did I even give her the camera? I know how irresponsible she is." She slapped her forehead. "Stupid, stupid, stupid."

Taylor and Eric walked up behind them. Melissa glared at them.

"We only shot a couple of minutes," Taylor said. "Give me the camera. I'll play it and prove it to you."

"Uh . . . the battery's dead. Remember?"

Taylor looked at her blankly for a second. "Oh."

Melissa turned to Daley. "What are you going to do about it?"

Daley blinked. "Me? Why me?"

"You want to be the leader," Melissa said hotly. "Lead!"

Daley looked at Taylor and Eric, then at Melissa. Her face was as blank as Taylor's.

"Great," Melissa said.

"Look!" Lex said. They had reached a swampy area. Bugs flittered through the heavy, moist air. The air smelled of mud and decay. There were no trees now, just high marsh grass.

"What?" Jackson said.

"See?" He pointed at shoe prints.

Jackson walked over and knelt down by the prints. "Looks like he was walking this way." He pointed across the marsh toward a stand of coconut palms.

"I bet he was going for those coconuts," Lex said. He started to cross the marsh.

Jackson held up one hand, instructing Lex to wait, then pointed at the mud.

Lex looked to see what Jackson was indicating. There were a series of indentations next to the shoe prints.

"What are those?"

"Hoof prints," Jackson said.

Jackson was right. Lex looked more closely. They were split-toed prints. "Looks like a deer," Lex said.

Jackson shook his head.

"Then what?"

"Wild hogs."

"Pigs? Cool. We could eat them, couldn't we? I mean . . . if we could catch them."

Jackson didn't say anything.

"What?" Lex said.

Jackson's eyes were glued to the high grass in front of them. Lex tried to see if anything was moving. But you could have a hidden a car in that grass and nobody would have been able to see it.

"I read in a book once," Lex said, "that a big male can rip your guts open with his tusks. Maybe we should—"

Jackson held his finger to his lips, picked up the sharp stick that he'd been carrying, then motioned for Lex to get behind him. He started crossing the marsh.

"What do you want me to do, Melissa?" Daley said. She spread her hands out helplessly.

Taylor and Eric looked at each other. Eric had a funny expression on his face, like there was something he wasn't saying. He probably knew exactly what Taylor had done. But Melissa knew that he wouldn't say so: It was totally obvious he was all gaga about Taylor and wouldn't do anything that might make her look bad.

"She can't get away with this," Melissa said.

"I didn't do anything!" Taylor said.

"Other than ruin the camera, no."

"All I did was use it, just like you."

"Then how come the battery's dead?"

"I don't know! I'm not, like . . . some scientist or something."

"What are you gonna do, Daley?" Melissa demanded.

"Yeah," Taylor said. "What *are* you gonna do?"

Daley swallowed, looked back and forth from Taylor to Melissa. Eric was looking up at the trees like he'd developed a sudden interest in biology.

"Uh . . ." Daley said. "I gotta go to the bathroom."

Then she rushed off. It was obvious to Melissa that she was just trying to avoid taking any responsibility for straightening things out.

Melissa threw up her hands. This was really upsetting.

Eric watched Melissa stomp off in one direction as Daley slipped off in the other. Taylor sashayed away toward the beach. Eric was left standing by himself. He looked around and then shook his head. All this drama over a freaking battery the size of his pinkie finger.

"Is it me?" he said. "Or is this getting kinda blown out of proportion?"

There was no answer from the empty jungle.

Wonder where Nathan is? he thought. *Seems like it's kinda been a while.*

Lex and Jackson tiptoed into the coconut grove. Lex listened for the sound of a pig. He imagined some huge razorback with little red eyes staring at them, its tusks flecked with blood.

Instead they saw nothing.

Jackson had his spear up like he was ready to stab anything that moved. Suddenly he held up his hand and froze.

Lex's heart started beating fast. "What?" he whispered.

Jackson cupped his hand behind his ear, listening.

Lex shook his head. He didn't hear anything.

Jackson turned slowly, the point of his spear tracking in front of him.

Then Lex heard it. Something rustling on the other side of a huge palm tree.

"What do you think it is?" Lex whispered.

Jackson put his hand to his lips. For a moment he hesitated. Then he started creeping forward toward the noise.

There it was again. A soft rustling sound. It couldn't be Nathan. There was nothing on the other side of the tree but a little bush. If Nathan had been standing behind the bush, they'd have seen him.

Jackson froze again. Lex could see his knuckles white against the spear. Man—if a tough guy like Jackson was nervous, then . . .

The rustling stopped. There was probably some huge killer hog on the other side of the bush, watching them and sharpening its tusks, waiting for the right moment to charge.

Suddenly Jackson burst into a run. "Ahhhhhhhh!" he yelled. He was brandishing his spear now.

Lex didn't know anything to do but follow. He grabbed a stick off the ground, held it up like Jackson, and ran.

"Yahhhhhhhh!!!!" Lex yelled.

"Ahhhhhhhhhhhhhh!" Jackson yelled.

Jackson leaped over the bush, his spear ready to strike. Lex knew he couldn't vault the bush so he ran around it, fully expecting to see Jackson going face-to-face with a crazed hog.

Instead, he saw . . .

Nathan.

Lying on the ground on his back.

Jackson stopped, spear still upraised, looking like he was about to stab Nathan in the chest.

"Is he alive?" Lex said.

Jackson didn't answer. They both stared at the motionless figure.

Suddenly Nathan moved feebly, the palm frond rustling underneath him. Then his eyes opened. He squinted up at Jackson.

"You don't need to kill me," Nathan said. "I think I'm already dead."

Lex and Jackson started laughing. "Guess he's alive," Lex said.

"Barely," Nathan said. He sat up, rubbing the back of his head. "Oh, man, I was lying there thinking I was gonna wake up at home in my bed."

"What happened to you?" Lex said.

Nathan kept rubbing his head. "I fell out of the palm tree."

Jackson and Lex looked up at the tall tree towering over them. "*That* tree?" Jackson said.

"I was trying to get coconuts."

"Cool," Lex said. "I'm kind of hungry. How many coconuts did you get?"

Nathan sat up, looked around. "Uh . . ."

"Wait a minute," Jackson said. "You went off into the jungle all by yourself, climbed up some giant tree without any safety rope or anything, and nearly killed yourself? And after all that, you got zero coconuts?"

Nathan stood unsteadily. "Yeah, but it proves how far I'm willing to go for you guys."

"Or how dumb you are," Jackson said.

Nathan rubbed his head and winced.

EIGHTEEN

Melissa stood near the door of the plane. All the others sat around her in a semicircle—except for Jackson, who leaned against the plane, sharpening the point of his spear with his long knife. It was getting late in the afternoon, but the sun was still high in the sky, beating down on them. Melissa took one last look at the trees to see if Captain Russell was going to appear. It was becoming almost like a reflex with her, checking to see if help—or at least some answers—was emerging from the jungle. And once again . . . nothing there.

Finally she intentionally turned her back on the jungle.

"Everybody?" Melissa said. "Um, okay? So Captain Russell's still not back. There aren't any boats out there, no planes flying over, no friendly villagers wandering out of the jungle. How long are we going to be here? I don't know. But it could be a while. And if we don't start all rowing in the same direction . . . well, it's just not gonna be good. Right?"

There were nods around the circle.

"So I guess it's time to go ahead with the vote. We gave Daley and Nathan the chance to prove who should be our leader. So before we vote, they're each going to get to argue their case. First up is Daley."

Melissa sat and Daley stood up, cleared her throat. She looked calm and composed. "Hi. I want to be your leader because we're in a tough situation and if we're going to survive, we need to be organized. Captain Russell might show up in ten minutes with help. Then again, I don't mean to scare everybody, but for all we know, he might never come back. Just to be on the safe side, I think we need to assume the worst. Which means we have to be disciplined and organized, so we can hold out until help arrives." She spoke slowly and methodically, like she had written out her speech and memorized it.

"I can keep us organized. And I'll prove it with my rationing plan." She pointed to two large plastic bins. "I spent the day making an inventory of all the food and water we have. It's mostly dried stuff, but it's got calories. With my ration plan, I'm happy to say we're in pretty good shape."

Daley glanced at Lex. Lex frowned back at her. Melissa wondered what was up with that. It made her feel a little nervous. Was there something Daley wasn't telling them? Something that only Lex knew?

"I made a menu," Daley continued, "balancing carbs and fats and protein so that we all have a solid diet of around a thousand calories a day. If we stick to it—"

"Wait a minute," Eric said. "A thousand calories! That's like nothing."

"It's plenty to sustain life. We may experience occasional feelings of ... uh ... inanition."

"Inane-what?" Taylor said.

"Hunger," Jackson said. "The word means *hunger*."

Everybody looked at Jackson for a moment.

"Hunger? Well, why didn't you say so?" Nathan said. "Wait, so . . . let me get this straight. Your plan to feed us will make us hungry. That's very ingenious. Very subtle."

Daley gave the group a strained smile. "Do you suppose my opponent would let me finish my speech?"

"Excuse *me*," Nathan said. "By all means, finish your oration."

"As I was saying," Daley said, "a thousand calories is enough to sustain us. If we stick to my plan and conserve water, I think we can last a long time."

"How long?" Lex said.

Daley smiled at her younger brother. It was the sort of smile, Melissa reflected, that you gave somebody when you really wanted them to shut up.

"Pardon me?" Daley said.

"How long will the food last?"

Daley cleared her throat. "Um. Well. See, we could be rescued anytime. So I'd have to say, long enough."

"Didn't you just say we had to assume the worst?" Lex pursued.

"We'll be fine." Daley gave him a condescending smile. "Anyone else?"

Nathan raised his hand. "May I ask a question?"

"Sure, Nathan." Daley's voice was full of exaggerated politeness.

"You rationed both the food and the water?"

"Yes. Separately."

"And did you calculate how much water we'll need to make the dried food?"

Daley didn't move. It was obvious from the deer-in-the-headlights expression on her face that she hadn't figured into her calculations the water needed to prepare the food.

"Well," she said finally. "That's a good point. But I don't think it'll be a huge amount."

Melissa noticed Lex shaking his head with a disgusted expression on his face.

Taylor held up her hand, waved it around. "And, um, what are you going to do about people who blame other people for stuff they didn't do?"

Melissa felt herself getting mad all over again. "But you did do it!"

"No, I didn't!"

"What happened?" Lex said.

"Taylor ran down the batteries on the video camera," Melissa said.

"I did not!"

"Well, somebody did."

Jackson slapped his hand on the side of the plane. It made a hollow boom. Everyone shut up and looked at him.

"You're all twisted because somebody ran some batteries down? On a *video camera?*"

Melissa suddenly felt stupid. "Well . . ."

"I didn't do it," Taylor said. "I need that camera. I've got B.O., and that's the only way to prove it."

Everyone looked confused. *B.O.?* Melissa thought. *What's Taylor babbling about?*

"Talk to the little guy," Jackson said, pointing his spear at Lex.

"Who, Lex?" Daley said.

"Tell 'em," Jackson said.

Lex stood up and showed them a black shiny-looking panel with little squares all over the front of it.

"I found this on *Twenty-Nine Down,*" Lex said. "It's got a series of two dozen single crystal silicon solar cells. I think it's a newer model because it's even got a blocking diode and this totally cool—"

"I'm sure," Eric interrupted, "that everyone is just, like, *massively* excited about this news. I know I am. But I think I speak for the whole group when I say: 'Huh?' "

"It's a battery charger. Solar-powered." Lex held up the panel so it faced toward the sun. "We can recharge the camera and any other batteries that are rechargeable. Like the camping lights."

"Lex, that is awesome," Nathan said, giving the younger boy a high five.

"See?" Taylor said, glaring at Melissa. "I knew it wasn't a problem."

Nathan stood. "If you're finished, Daley . . ."

She shrugged. "Go ahead."

Nathan smiled confidently at the group. "I'm sure Daley worked real hard on her feeding schedule. I, for one, appreciate her work." He paused, raised one eyebrow. "But hey. Guys. Let's think big picture, huh? How long are we gonna be here? We have no idea. I mean that's the one thing Daley and I agree about. We have to assume the worst. At a minimum, we have to assume that Captain Russell may take a while to get back with help. We need a leader who looks forward, not back. What I did was go out into the jungle, blaze a trail, find out what potential food sources are out there. For the future. That way we're gonna have food even when our provisions run out."

"Yeah. And?" Eric said.

Nathan grinned. "Dude, I found more food out in the jungle than we could ever need."

Everybody looked at each other.

"Awesome," Taylor said. "So where is it?"

Nathan's grin faded. "Well. You know. Out there." He pointed at the jungle.

"You mean you didn't *get any*?" Eric said. "I'm hungry!"

"Well, true, I haven't got any just this minute. But the reason I didn't is because—"

"Because you fell out of a tree!" Daley said. "What if

you'd gotten killed? Where would that leave us?"

Nathan looked at the ground.

Daley turned to the group. "Is that the kind of leader we want? A loose cannon who goes off on his own little tangent, needs to be rescued . . . and then doesn't even deliver?"

"Or do we want somebody who needs her little brother to accomplish anything productive?" Nathan said.

"So where are the coconuts? Or did you just imagine them?" Daley retorted.

"And how much food *do* we have, Daley?" Nathan retorted. "I noticed you were pretty quick to dodge Lex's question. What aren't you telling us?"

"Maybe you should have asked for help instead of trying to act like some cowboy hero."

Daley and Nathan were both standing now, getting in each other's faces. Melissa wanted to go crawl in a hole. She hated what was happening to them. Daley was usually so calm and reasonable. And Nathan was normally the nicest guy she knew. Now look at them. And the tension rubbed off on everybody.

"And maybe you should have been looking for water instead of sitting around counting things and making cute little lists on a clipboard . . ."

"And maybe they should have left you out there . . ."

"And maybe . . ."

Jackson walked between the two, pushed them apart. "Enough," he said. Then he turned to Melissa.

Something about his manner made her feel calmer. It was like he wasn't letting the uncertainty of this whole business get to him. And his assurance seemed to rub off on her, to make her feel more confident about herself. Why couldn't Daley and Nathan be like that? It seemed like all their bickering just made everybody else feel more scared, more nervous. It was like Jackson could see what mattered and what didn't. Once you stopped worrying about things that didn't matter, everything seemed more doable.

Melissa took a deep breath, then looked around the group. No one spoke.

"Okay then," Melissa said. "I guess we're ready to vote. I'll give each of you a piece of paper. Write the name of whoever you vote for on it, then fold it up and put it in this box." She held up a small plastic box salvaged from the plane. "Vote for the person you want to be our leader. Whoever wins, we gotta go with them. That's the deal. No more arguments."

Jackson looked around the group, his eyes pausing significantly on both Daley and Nathan. "From anybody."

Melissa set the box in the middle of the circle.

"There are seven pencils in here," she said. "Help yourself."

Everybody picked up a pencil, sat down, and looked thoughtfully into the air. After a minute, they all began to write.

NINETEEN

Lex

Static.

Okay, I know I'm the nerdy little kid who's into all the technical stuff. I know everybody gets all bored with it. But I can't help it.

You know what static is. A lot of people use the word "static" to mean "fighting."

But static also means that noise kssshhhhhhhhhh— that you hear when a radio isn't tuned to a station. If you wiggle your finger up in the air like this, see? That's what a radio wave looks like. Or a sound wave. Or a TV broadcast signal. It's just energy, jiggling around.

But when the energy is jiggling along in one direction, you can bounce a radio signal across the entire world. Isn't that cool? Well, it is to me anyway.

But when the jiggling isn't coordinated? Noise. Static on your radio. Snow on your TV. Random stuff.

Kssssssshhhhhhhhhhhhhhhhhhhhhhhhhhhhhhhhhhhhh.

That's what it's like right now. Static.

We need a signal. We need a direction. Because right now everybody's all jiggling around like crazy, and we're just banging into each other. Our food's running out. Our water's running out. And we're starting to get on one another's nerves.

You ever read that book, *Lord of the Flies*? Where these kids get marooned on this island and they end up ... well, I don't even want to say what they end up doing to one another.

Yeah. I know. I don't want to think about it.

Static. Too much static.

Melissa picked up the box, counted the slips of paper. "Four ... five ... six ... seven ..."

Melissa opened each slip of paper, stacked them up, read the votes. She looked up and frowned. This was kind of surprising. Daley and Nathan were fidgeting nervously.

"Well, do we have a leader?" Taylor said.

"I *think* so," Melissa said.

"You think so?" Nathan said. "Who won?"

"Well, one person voted for nobody."

She held up a blank slip of paper. She looked around the circle. Everybody was looking slightly puzzled or irritated— everyone except Jackson, who appeared vaguely bored by the whole thing. She had a hunch she knew who the blank paper came from.

"Is that legal?" Taylor said.

Melissa held up another slip of paper. "One person voted for Nathan."

"Wait a minute." Nathan stared at her. "Only one?"

Melissa nodded.

Nathan looked crushed. Then his eyes narrowed slightly as he realized that meant that even Melissa hadn't voted for him. He looked at her accusingly. Melissa looked away.

Daley jumped up, pumped her fists in the air. "Yes!"

"You might want to hold off on the victory lap, Daley," Melissa said. "You only got one vote, too." She held up another piece of paper, this one with Daley's neat handwriting on it.

Daley's posture sagged a little. Everyone in the group looked puzzled.

"I don't get it," Daley said.

Melissa waved the last four ballots in the air. "The deal was we'd all accept the vote. No argument."

"But if four people didn't vote . . ." Nathan said.

"But they did," Melissa said. "Four people voted for the person they most wanted to be our leader. That person was . . ."

Everyone waited. Out in the forest a bird called raucously. The waves thumped the beach.

". . . Jackson."

TWENTY

"**J**ackson?" Daley said.

"Jackson! But—" Nathan turned and looked at Jackson. Jackson looked expressionlessly back at him.

"He wasn't even running!" Daley said in an aggrieved tone of voice.

"It's not fair!" Nathan said.

Eric started laughing, "Nah, perfect is what it is."

"And it's what we agreed to," Melissa added.

"Yeah, but . . . but . . ." Daley spluttered.

"Save it," Jackson said. "I don't want the job."

Melissa watched as he started walking away. For a moment she thought maybe it would be best to let him go. But then she looked at Daley and Nathan's faces, at the way they were getting all pumped up for a big battle, and suddenly she felt like Jackson was their only hope.

"Jackson! Wait!" she called.

But he just kept walking.

Around her everyone was talking.

"Organized chaos," Eric said. "I love it."

"Who voted for Jackson?" Daley demanded. "I want to know."

"Well, duh," Nathan said. "It's not hard to figure out."

"But why? This is insane." Daley looked around the circle. "How could you people want him to be the leader? While he was sitting around acting all Johnny Depp, I figured out a rationing plan that's gonna help us survive!" She reached into the tub where the water was stored. "If you think that doesn't count, then . . ." Her eyes widened. "Uh-oh."

"What's the matter?" Lex said.

Daley stared for several seconds, then said softly, "No way."

"What is it, Daley?" Melissa said.

"Some of our drinking water is gone."

"What do you mean, gone?" Nathan demanded.

"I mean I put everything we had in here. Every last bottle. Six are missing. That means . . ."

"It means somebody's a thief," Lex said.

"And if we don't get them back, we're going to run out of water a lot quicker than I thought." Daley slammed the lid of the plastic bin shut, looked around the circle of faces. "This is no joke, guys. Who took the water?"

"What's the big deal?" Taylor said. "You said we had plenty for a while. Right?"

Daley looked off at the surf, an uncomfortable look on her face.

"Oh no . . ." Nathan said. "How long is 'a while,' Daley?"

She rubbed her face nervously. "Well, I figured if we each drank a couple of pints a day, and ate a thousand calories, the food and water would last the seven of us for . . . uh . . ."

"Well?"

". . . three more days."

Nathan threw up his hands in disgust. "Oh, for—"

"You're kidding!" Eric said.

"That's not possible!" Taylor said.

Melissa looked down the beach. Jackson was still walking away from them, his sharpened stick leaving little holes in the sand as he walked. He'd started the fire after letting Nathan make a fool of himself. He'd stepped in—what?—two or three times to chill people out when things were getting hairy between other kids. All the problems and challenges they were facing and he'd never once gotten flustered, never once freaked out about anything. He seemed to be the only one who wasn't scared. Did he have the answers to their other problems locked up in his mysterious head? If so, he wasn't saying. What else was he holding back? He got smaller and smaller, walking down the beach in no apparent hurry. How could he be so calm when the whole situation was so messed up?

After a minute the group quieted down.

"Look, anyway, what's the big deal?" Taylor said. "Three days, that's like forever. No way we're gonna be here another three days."

Everybody glared at her.

"Right?" Taylor said. "Right?"

Lex shook his head. Eric looked up in the air. Daley rolled her eyes.

"So, Daley," Lex said, "now that six bottles are missing, where does that leave us? Can we still make it for three days?"

"If we each drink a pint a day."

"A pint!" Nathan said. "In a day? Come on, I drink more than a pint during one football practice."

"And what about if Captain Russell and the others come back?" Melissa said.

"*When* Captain Russell comes back," Taylor said.

"If," Melissa said.

"We're getting off track," Eric said.

"But seriously," Nathan said. "Let's say they walk in here five minutes from now. How many days?"

"Uh . . . They took food and water with them."

"Three days worth?"

Daley shook her head. Her mouth was firm, but her eyes were looking red-rimmed, like she might cry any minute. "I don't know," she whispered. "I just don't know."

Everybody looked around suspiciously. Melissa wondered who might have taken the water. Six bottles? That was not a minor thing. Could it have been Eric and Taylor? She looked down the beach. What about Jackson? He was so hard to read. There had been rumors about him back at school, about how he was some kind of juvenile delinquent and stuff. She couldn't believe he'd do a thing like this. So far he seemed like a pretty cool guy. But still . . .

Nathan stood up. "Okay, guys. Whoever took the water, fess up. We didn't know the situation before. Now we do. Give back the water—no harm, no foul."

Nobody moved. Nobody spoke.

"What about Jackson?" Daley said.

"I'll ask him about it," Melissa said.

"People!" Daley said. "Hello? We're in trouble here."

"Let's not get crazy," Nathan said. "I think we should start looking for fresh water on the island."

Everyone nodded. They all stood up. Except for Eric.

"Hold up," Eric said. "What about the election? Who's in charge?"

Nathan and Daley looked at each other.

"I guess we both are," Nathan said.

"Great," Eric said. "Now I feel really safe."

TWENTY-ONE

Nathan

Unbelievable. They voted for Jackson.

Yeah, Jackson! I mean, for a minute I was ticked at him. But the more I thought about it, the more I can't blame everybody for voting for him. Daley and I were being pretty jerky. Though I'd never admit that to her. It's not good for the group.

But now with this water thing, I've got a chance to prove what I can really do. That's my goal. I'm gonna be the one to find water.

Uh. I hope.

Daley was moving the last of the provisions from the campsite back to the plane. Lex trailed behind her with one of the extra sleeping bags.

"Where do you want this?" Lex said.

"Don't talk to me," Daley snapped, throwing the box she was carrying on the ground next to the plane.

"Come on, Daley," Lex said.

"I can't believe you didn't vote for me."

Lex sighed. It was a little awkward. "I'm sorry. I didn't know anybody else would vote for Jackson."

"So what? You're my little brother."

"Yeah, and that's exactly what you've been treating me like. Some little kid who's not worth taking seriously."

"I take you seriously. I just—"

"Look, it was a protest vote, okay?"

"So you undermined me just because I'm a little stressed? Because I didn't cozy up to you the whole time and pat you on the head every time you did something good?"

"No, that's not it. The problem was, you and Nathan aren't acting like leaders."

For a minute Lex thought she would argue with him. But then her anger appeared to dissipate and she plunked down on the sand, putting her chin on her hands. "I want to go home, Lex," she said. "I want pizza. I want to hear music. I want to see Mom and Dad. I hate not having music. I think that's the worst part. It's so . . . quiet."

Lex tried to be reassuring. He put his arm around her neck. "We'll get home soon."

His sister stiffened, stood up sharply. "Don't talk to me."

Lex

I feel like a traitor. Sort of. I mean, Daley's really angry. And scared. She doesn't show it—but I guess we all have ways of covering it up.

Well, one good thing, there was another battery for

the video camera. So we don't have to wait for the solar charger to finish charging up the batteries. These video diaries are a good idea. They help blow off steam. I hope Daley makes one. She's not exactly good at stress relief. And I don't think she really has anyone to talk to. She's so busy being tough that she kind of drives people away from her. That's sad. She's really okay when you get to know her. I mean... most of the time she is.

Well, anyway, she gave me an idea. I better go get busy...

Daley kept staring angrily at the bin where the water was stored. Who took the water? She couldn't believe somebody would be that inconsiderate. No, inconsiderate was not nearly strong enough. Their lives were at stake. Taking six bottles of water bordered on being evil.

She went over and looked at the ground around the bin. Maybe the perpetrator had left footprints.

After a careful study of the sand, she gave up on that idea. There were about a million prints in the sand. It could have been anybody.

She picked up the lid, looked inside. Maybe she had just miscounted. She counted once, twice, a third time.

Nope. Not that she was incapable of making a mistake. But miscounting by six bottles? That wasn't Daley Marin. She put the lid on slowly.

As she closed the lid, she noticed something slippery on her fingers. She felt her brow furrowing. What was it? Did it mean something?

She lifted her fingers to her nose and sniffed. Then she looked angrily down the beach.

"Coppertone!" she said.

Nathan unrolled one of the extra tents, pulled out the rain fly—a big sheet of nylon cloth that was used to keep rain off the tent—and began setting it up on the sand near the edge of the forest. He'd done this for his merit badge, so he knew it could be done.

Eric ambled up as he was getting started.

"Whatcha doing?" Eric said.

"It's a rain catcher," Nathan said.

He was trying to get all the poles up so that he could angle the fly: one corner high, the far corner low. Unfortunately the wind kept turning the fly into a sail and blowing it around so it knocked over the poles. Eric stood with his hands behind his back, not offering to help as the fly blew over and the poles got all tangled.

"You noticed it's kind of falling over?" Eric said.

Nathan grunted. "The idea is that when it rains, the water will run down the fly, collect in this little crease here, and flow into that cup. Ta-da! Drinking water!"

"The cup that's blowing away in the wind, you mean?" Eric said. He watched as the small plastic cup that Nathan had set on the ground at the far end of the rain catcher went spinning across the beach.

"You think you could get that?" Nathan said.

"Oh. I mean, I guess so," Eric said. He trotted across the sand, picked up the cup, walked slowly back. By that point Nathan had the fly secured. Eric handed him the cup and Nathan jammed it down into the sand.

"So," Eric said. "A rain catcher, huh? Nice."

"Thanks."

Eric nodded knowingly, then looked up at the sky. Nathan followed his gaze toward the sky. It was blue and clear—and totally cloudless.

"And how do you get it to rain?" Eric said.

"It'll rain," Nathan said.

Eric frowned. "And . . . what if it doesn't?"

Nathan felt the air go out of his lungs. For a guy who never did anything, Eric was sure good at making other people feel stupid. Problem was, in this case he was right. No rain, no water. In which case his carefully constructed rain catcher was worthless.

Nathan scowled, then started ripping the poles out of the sand.

"I got a better idea," he said.

Eric stood back watching, hands behind his back, a faint smile on his face.

Melissa found Jackson sitting under a tree about half a mile down the beach. He was whittling on his spear with his big knife. She sat down next to him. For a while neither of them spoke. From here Melissa couldn't see the other kids at all. For a minute it felt almost like they were the only two people on the island. It gave Melissa a weird feeling—half lonely and frightened, half excited. There was something about Jackson that intrigued her. She couldn't put her finger on what it was though. She watched him slice away at the wood for a while.

"You're gonna turn that thing into a toothpick pretty soon," Melissa said finally.

Jackson shrugged. "Plenty more where this came from."

"Somebody stole a bunch of our water."

Jackson looked up at her, surprised. His mouth twisted angrily, then he stabbed his stick into the sand. "Unbelievable."

Melissa pulled the stick out of the sand, felt the point. It was needle sharp. "Why don't you want to be the leader?" she said.

He didn't answer, just reached over, took the stick back from her, and started whittling again.

"I know Captain Russell will be back eventually. I *hope* he will. But it's been kind of a long time and what if . . ."

Jackson said nothing.

"I think you'd be good," Melissa said. "You don't get caught up in all the drama. You're like—solid. If there's one thing we need right now, it's solid." She smiled a little. "That and water."

Jackson started peeling bark off the stick.

"I voted for you," Melissa said. She wasn't sure why, but she felt a little embarrassed admitting it. Like she'd just told him she thought he was cute or something.

He didn't react like she expected. Instead of seeming flattered, he looked irritated.

"I don't like people who tell other people what to do." He stood up, brushed the sand off the seat of his pants. "End of story."

He walked up the beach, heading even farther away from the group.

Melissa

So. Jackson. I talked to him today, tried to convince him to be the leader, but it's like he's just checking out on us.

I think there's a lot going on with Jackson. I mean, everybody at Hartwell has heard the rumors. He's supposedly from some crummy neighborhood. His father died in some kind of tragic way. His mom's supposedly in jail. He was in a gang. Or maybe he's even *still* in a gang. He's been in juvie for holding up grocery stores or beating up old ladies or whatever. I mean—it could all be bogus. Or not. Nobody really seems to know anything about him.

I think there's a lot going on inside him. A lot that he won't let out. Maybe that's why he seems angry all the time. I want to get to know him, but he doesn't let anybody inside.

Maybe—maybe I can change that.

Lex was in the cockpit, working. He felt happier than he'd felt since they hit the ground. Around him were dials and gauges and wires and pieces of electronic equipment. This was going to be an interesting challenge.

He climbed under the pilot's seat, studied the underside of the controls until he found a green wire that went into the back of the RF amplifier. He clipped it in half, pulled the wire out, stripped the end, attached it to a small electronic device the size of a dinner plate.

He hummed to himself.

He sure hoped this would work.

Hey, what was he thinking? Of course it would work. He'd *make* it work!

Daley was walking up the beach, still thinking about the water. Who was the thief? The whole thing chafed her like crazy. All her work was for nothing if some jerk was just going to steal the stuff as soon as she got everything inventoried and planned. Sure, she'd made a mistake giving away the bottles to Taylor and Eric in hopes that they'd vote for her. But that was a momentary lapse in judgment that wouldn't happen again.

And, hey, let's face it—it wasn't just about her. What if the group really *did* start running out of water before they got rescued? Whoever stole that water was endangering everybody else's life. This was no joke. It went beyond a mean prank or a stupid mistake. This was malicious. Worst case? Somebody could die because of it!

The way Daley figured it, the thief had to be one of three people. Taylor, Eric, or Jackson. Jackson was an unknown quantity. But there were a lot of stories about him. And Eric? Eric was a snake. He never got into confrontations with anybody, but you always knew he was working his own little agenda. And Taylor? All Taylor thought about was Taylor.

Daley saw something lying on the sand. She scooped it up. It was a pair of shorts. A few more yards and she saw a shirt. She recognized it as Taylor's. She picked it up, too. After a minute, she found a pair of sandals. Apparently Taylor was ditching all her clothes. Daley followed the line of discarded clothes.

As Daley kept walking, she heard singing. Off-key. It was coming from somewhere back in the jungle. Right about the place where Taylor's last piece of clothing lay on the sand.

Daley followed the sound of the out-of-tune singing. Within thirty seconds she stepped out from behind a tree.

There was Taylor, back to Daley, washing her hair. A bottle of water lay at her feet.

"Busted!" Daley said loudly.

Taylor screamed and whirled around.

"God, you scared me!" Taylor said.

Daley reached down and grabbed the water bottle. "Are you completely out of your mind, Taylor? Washing your *hair*?"

Taylor pawed at the lather covering her face. "I couldn't

take it anymore!" she whined. "My hair was starting to feel like that fake grass they put in Easter baskets."

"Taylor." Daley put on her most condescending tone of voice. "Did you happen to notice that we're stranded on a desert island with no water? Hm? And if we run out, did it cross your mind that we will all die?"

Taylor kept rubbing her face. "Hey, I'm dying right now!" Taylor said. "Give me the water. My eyes are burning!" She held her hand out, waving it around like a blind person.

Daley glared at her. "I hope they fry. Did you use all six bottles?"

"No!" Taylor's hand continued to paw at the air. "I took only one bottle, I swear! I didn't think it was that big a deal."

"I don't believe you."

"I'm serious. I took only one bottle. Daley, please. It burns!"

"Who took the rest?"

Taylor's hand stopped moving in the air. One corner of her mouth turned up. "If I tell you, will you give me some water?"

"No. But I'll lead you down to the ocean and you can rinse off there."

"But—"

"*Who took the water?*" Daley yelled.

Taylor kept shaking her head and pawing at the air, a childish whimpering noise coming out of her lips.

Nathan

Okay, Plan B. My rain catcher would have worked if there'd been rain. Unfortunately, no sign of that. So now I'm going to make a solar still. Simple idea. Solar stills take moisture out of the air. All you have to do is condense moisture from the air onto a surface, let it run down into a collector—and voilà! Drinking water.

The sun does all the work while you sit back and watch.

At least ... that's the theory. I've never actually seen one work. But it will. I think. I hope!

Nathan studied the beach to see where he should dig. To make the solar still, he needed to dig a cone-shaped pit in the sand. Once the pit was made, he'd cover it with plastic. Then above it he would erect the tent fly for the water to condense on. As the water condensed, it would run or drip down the sides of the fly into the cone. Then from there it would run into the center of the cone where it would collect.

It was going to be some work. But he didn't mind. Since football season was over, he'd been getting out of shape anyway. A little exercise would hit the spot.

He got a dinky camp shovel from the plane and then started digging. The work was a lot harder and slower than he'd expected. The walls of the pit kept caving in. Grit blew in his face. And the sand—man, it was heavy! He started wishing he had some help.

Eric appeared out of the trees, walking rapidly toward the plane. There was something furtive about the way he was moving, like he didn't want anybody to see him.

"Hey, Eric," Nathan called. "Looking for something to do?"

Eric looked surprised. "Huh? What?" He cupped his hand in front of his ear like he couldn't hear very well.

Nathan held up the shovel. "It's great exercise!"

Eric smiled broadly at him. "I'd love to, but I'm pretty busy with the—" Whatever it was that he was supposedly busy with, it was lost in the sound of the waves. Nathan suspected that he was mumbling on purpose.

"I could really use the help."

"I know. But I need to do the, you know, the thing that . . . I'm doing right now." He pointed vaguely at the plane, then gave Nathan a big thumbs-up. "You're doing great though. Keep it up!"

Eric turned and hurriedly disappeared back into the jungle. The only time he seemed to hurry was when he was avoiding work.

Nathan looked around the beach for somebody else who might be able to help. Lex was over by the airplane working intently on some kind of electronic equipment. Nathan was about to call for him, but then Lex disappeared back into the airplane. Besides, now that Nathan thought about it, everything Lex had done so far had turned out to be pretty smart and pretty useful. Might as well let the kid keep working on—well—whatever it was he was working on.

Nathan stabbed the sand with his shovel and sat down. He was breathing hard and his arms—already sore from his unsuccessful fire-starting efforts—were killing him. He wiped his face. He was sweating up a storm now. Man, what he wouldn't do for a drink of water!

Lex was working in the cockpit when he heard something creaking in the back of the plane. Like somebody was sneaking onto the plane, trying not to make any noise.

Lex poked his head out into the cabin. It was Eric.

"Hey!" Lex said.

Eric jumped, nearly hitting his head on the low ceiling of the plane. He whipped around, eyes wide. "Oh!" he said. "It's you. What are you doing in here?"

Lex held up some wires. "Depolarizing the battery contacts to make sure they're grounded in case of another storm."

"Oh. Yeah." Eric gave him his standard insincere smile.

"That was gonna be my second guess. So look, you gonna be long?"

Lex looked at Eric suspiciously. What was he up to? "Maybe. Why?"

Eric shrugged. "Just asking." Then he ducked back out of the cabin.

Daley saw Eric backing out of the plane. She was fuming. She ran up behind him and grabbed him by the arm.

"Where is it?" she demanded.

Eric turned around and looked at her with his usual innocent expression. "Where's what?"

Daley's eyes narrowed. "Don't lie to me, Eric. Taylor already told me you're the one who took the water."

She could see the wheels turning in Eric's mind, trying to figure out how he could weasel his way out of the situation. Apparently he came up dry, though, because his shoulders slumped a little and he said, "I guess you can't trust anybody."

"Yeah, tell me about it. I can see Taylor doing something like that because she's, well, she's an idiot. But you! Are you really so self-centered that you'd hurt the rest of us?"

Eric looked vaguely hurt. "It was a mistake, alright? As soon as I found out how bad off we really were, I was gonna put it back. That's why I was checking out the plane just now. But Junior's in there."

"Yeah, right."

"Believe me or don't, I don't care. But it's true. Besides, this is all your fault."

Daley cocked her head. "This I have to hear."

"No, seriously. This morning you gave Taylor and me some water and made it sound like it was no big deal. Of course that was when you wanted our votes. But since you were being all casual, we thought that we had all the water we needed. Imagine my surprise when it turned out that wasn't the truth." Eric put a self-righteous expression on his face.

Daley flushed. She knew he was jerking her around. But still. He was right that she'd misled them about the water situation this morning.

"So feel free to tell everybody I took the water, Daley." He leaned a little closer, then looked around as though to make sure nobody was listening. "But then I'll have to tell them about your questionable campaign tactics."

Daley clamped her mouth shut, blew some air out her nose. Eric had her over a barrel.

"Or . . ." Eric said. "You can do the smart thing—keep quiet, and help me return the water. Your choice."

Daley tried to figure a way out of the box Eric had put her into. She didn't like to admit it, but this was exactly what Lex had warned her about when she gave them the bottles in the first place. Stuff like that always came back and bit you in the rear.

"Well?" Eric said.

"I'm *thinking*!"

Nathan was finally finished with the solar still. The tarp made a nice clean funnel running down into the center, where a black volcanic rock held it down. He'd ringed the edges of the tarp with more volcanic rocks. Nathan clapped his palms together, getting the sand off his hands. He had gotten blisters from all the shoveling. But it was done. And a nice neat job, too!

Taylor walked up as he was admiring his work.

"No clue," Taylor said.

"It's a solar still," Nathan said.

Taylor kept looking blankly at it. Finally she smiled and

gave a little dismissive shrug. "No clue."

Nathan smiled, then pointed at the sky. "See, the heat from the sun creates vapor from the cooler air below. The vapor sticks to the outside of the funnel, forming water that drips down and collects in a cup underneath."

Taylor didn't seem to have any more idea what was going on than she had before. She kind of shook her head a little. "No clue!" she said pleasantly.

"Doesn't matter what the technical details are." Nathan was feeling generous right now. It didn't bother him that she didn't get how it worked. She'd get the picture when she had a nice cool drink. "In a couple hours we'll have water."

Daley and Eric were hustling back from the direction of the camp to the plane. Daley carried a backpack. She could feel the water bottles shifting around inside. How had Eric managed to arrange it so that she was the one who was actually carrying the water?

Daley hated herself for doing this. But what were her alternatives? She'd look like a fool if Eric told everybody about the water she'd given them.

They were just out of the trees, closing in on the plane when Lex stepped out of the hatch of the DeHavilland. He had a long green wire trailing behind him.

She felt a momentary panic. If he busted them, she'd never hear the end of it. *I told you, Daley, but you didn't listen, blah blah blah*. She turned and headed back toward the jungle. Eric was already running for the trees.

When they reached a big gnarled tree on the other side of a dune, they stopped. Both of them were breathing hard.

"Whew!" Eric said. "This is too much like work."

"I'm the one carrying all the water," she said.

"Speaking of which, could you turn around?"

She started to turn around, but then realized that Eric was reaching for one of the bottles in the pack on her back. She whipped back around. "What is *wrong* with you?"

"What? I'm thirsty."

"We're all thirsty. Suck it up."

"Hey, I'm trying. But I have very sensitive blood sugar. In fact I feel kind of faint right now." He swayed a little bit like he was about to fall over.

Daley gave him the evil eye and he stopped swaying.

"I can't believe I'm doing this," Daley said.

"Look, as long as that little geek is doing whatever he's doing, we're never gonna get the water back. I say we just chug our share right now."

Daley frowned. The deeper she got into this, the more uncomfortable she felt.

"No," she said finally. "Not only are we not going to drink our share, we're going to make this right for everybody."

Eric looked at her like she'd just said they were going to fly to the moon. "How?"

"We're going to find fresh water."

She cinched the pack tighter on her back, then put her face close to Eric's. "And he's not a geek."

She turned and started walking into the jungle. Eric didn't move. She clapped her hands. "Hey! Eric. Chop-chop."

Eric sighed loudly, then followed her. It was time for Captain Russell to get back with help. Because this was turning out to be a real pain.

Daley

I feel so incredibly guilty about the whole thing. Eric's a rat . . . but I'm not any better. Still, I don't want the truth to come out, or nobody will ever trust me. The only way out of this is to make the whole problem go away. . . .

Eric followed Daley into the clearing and looked around. "Yeah, so?" he said.

"This is where I got attacked by leeches."

"Here?" Eric looked alarmed. "Right *here*?"

Daley shrugged. "Sure. Right here."

"Are you crazy?" Eric started hopping around on the spongy ground like he was expecting dozens of leeches to leap up out of the grass and start chomping on his legs. "What if they get on me?"

Daley let him hop around for a while. "Oh, stop," she said finally. "They can't get through your shoes."

"Oh." Eric stopped hopping around. He looked suspiciously at the ground. "Can they, like, crawl up your shoe or something?"

"They're worms, Eric. You ever had an earthworm jump up onto your leg?"

"No."

"Well, there you are then. Leeches are worms. They don't jump."

Eric kept looking nervously down at the grass. "So why are we here? Is this some kind of punishment?"

Daley bent down and poked the soggy grass. "Lex said that the leeches were here because the ground is damp. Feel that."

Eric laughed sharply. "No way. I'll take your word for it." He shrugged. "So what are we supposed to do—suck on the ground?"

"If the ground is damp," Daley said, "there's got to be water coming from somewhere. All we have to do is find the source."

She walked across the clearing. Eric started hopping comically after her. It was hard to know if he was serious or if he was just trying to come up with yet another reason not to do anything.

"Look!" she said. "Over there."

Melissa was tending the fire. It was starting to get late and the air off the ocean was cooling. She had had high hopes for the election—thinking that it would calm things down a little, get rid of all the tension and friction. But if anything, it had just made things worse. They needed to focus on surviving. And instead they were getting all distracted by these personal rivalries.

She was poking her fire stick disconsolately at the burning logs when she heard someone come up behind her.

She turned and found Jackson looking at her. He shuffled his feet awkwardly. She turned back to the fire.

"I'm sorry I went off on you, Melissa," Jackson said.

She shrugged and kept staring at the fire. "No problem," she said finally.

Jackson circled around the fire, sat down opposite her, and looked off at the darkening sky. It was obvious he had something to say. But he seemed to have trouble getting it to come out. Melissa figured she wouldn't push him.

Finally he said, "Power's a scary thing. Some people want it a little too much."

Melissa let out a thin, brief laugh. "Sounds familiar."

"For some people, control is everything . . . and they don't mind beating the snot out of other people to get it."

What was he talking about? Nathan and Daley might have been a pain in the neck—but they weren't fighting physically. He must be talking about something in his own life. But what? Something about his family? The kids he hung out with before he came to Hartwell? She had no idea.

Jackson shook his head sharply. "I hate people like that. I don't want to be like that. So let it go."

"Being our leader doesn't mean you have to beat people up or something. All we're talking about is somebody to help us get focused and stay organized."

"Power makes people do bad stuff. No thanks. Not interested."

"The thing is," Melissa said, "you don't *want* the power. That's exactly why you'd be so perfect for the job."

Jackson met her eye. There was something in there that intrigued her and scared her at the same time. She smiled.

Jackson kept looking at her. His face softened a little. But he didn't smile back. He seemed to be thinking about something.

Eric and Daley fought their way through vines and short, rubbery trees, moved all the way around the perimeter of the clearing, then climbed up a jumble of volcanic rock. Eric kept grumbling the whole time.

"What!" Eric said finally. "You pointed at something. You said, 'Look over there.' And now there's nothing. I don't see a thing."

Daley stopped. "I thought I saw something gleaming over here. Like water."

Eric slapped at a mosquito. "Well, there's nothing here."

Daley frowned and looked at the ground. "You just slapped a mosquito, right?"

Eric had a vexed expression on his face. "So?"

"Where do mosquitoes grow?"

Eric shrugged.

"Water!" Daley said. "*Think*, Eric. Mosquitoes grow in

standing water. If there's a mosquito here, it had to have grown someplace where there's water."

"So show it to me."

Daley looked around, frustrated. "It doesn't make sense, Eric. We've got mosquitoes. We've got damp ground. But no streams, no ponds, no nothing. Where in the world is it coming from?"

Eric shrugged like he didn't care. "Who knows, Daley," he said irritably. "Maybe it comes up out of the freakin' ground. How should I know?"

He started to walk away from her. Daley's eyes widened. Of course! That was it. All this volcanic rock on the island was probably full of underground caverns and stuff. And some of them were probably full of water that came down off the mountains and sank into the soil.

"That's it!" Daley said. "It's underground!"

"Yeah, right," Eric said.

"Go back to the camp!" Daley said excitedly. "There's something I need you to get . . ."

"Excellent!" Eric smiled broadly. "How'd I guess? More work."

"So . . . where do you live?" Melissa said.

"I don't like to talk about that," Jackson said.

"Why not?"

Jackson stared at the fire.

"I'm not a blabbermouth," Melissa said. "You can talk to me."

"I just don't feel real close to these guys," Jackson said. "They take everything for granted."

"That doesn't mean they're bad people."

Jackson shook his head. "Never said they were. I'm just saying I've been through some stuff that most of you guys probably wouldn't get."

Melissa didn't say anything. The truth was, she'd had a pretty easy life so far. She felt grateful for that. "Everybody thinks you're some kind of big criminal mastermind," Melissa said. "I mean, that's what the rumors were at school." She winced. "I don't mean me personally. *I* don't think that, but ..."

Jackson looked up at her sharply. "What if I was some big thug? Would you still want me to be the leader?"

"I ..." Melissa stuttered, not sure how to answer.

"Yeah. Didn't think so." Jackson tossed a twig into the fire.

"No," Melissa said. "You want to know the truth? I don't care. I don't care what you've done, where you come from, who your parents are. It just doesn't matter. We're here. Okay? What happened back there is back there."

Jackson looked at her thoughtfully.

For some reason, Melissa felt her face getting hot. After a few seconds Jackson just looked away and stared at the fire.

Daley ran back into the clearing, Eric trailing after her, breathing hard. He was carrying the camp shovel that Nathan had used to dig the solar still with.

"Man, it's getting dark out here," Eric said. "I think we should get back to camp."

"Quit complaining and start digging," Daley said.

Eric threw the shovel on the ground. "Help yourself," he said. "My blood sugar's getting out of whack again."

Daley snorted, picked up the shovel. Eric sat down on the ground for a moment, then lay back and closed his eyes.

"Is that a leech on your neck?" Daley said.

Eric leaped off the ground, started pawing at his neck. "Where? Where? Where?"

Daley laughed. "Oh, my mistake," she said.

Eric stopped grabbing at his neck. "Very funny," he said. "I hope you know I have a heart murmur, too. Your little joke could have caused me to go into cardiac arrest."

"I hear exercise is just the thing for people with weak hearts." She held out the shovel.

Eric pretended not to see it. He looked out at the jungle. "Maybe I should go sit on the beach and wait for Captain Russell," he said. "I mean, what if he gets back to the plane and we're not there?"

She was about to get into it with him—but the fact was you wasted more effort getting Eric to do anything than if you just did it yourself. So she jammed the shovel into the ground.

Eric looked at her skeptically. "What are you trying to do—dig a well?"

"Sort of."

"Sounds dumb to me."

"Look, the ground is wet. Right? So there has to be water in it. If I dig far enough . . ." She pushed on the blade of the shovel with her foot until it sank all the way into the ground. Then she levered up a chunk of soil and roots. It took a lot of work getting through the roots. Finally she lifted up her heavy load of soil, threw it to the side of the little hole. She looked in the hole. The soil appeared to be bone dry. Surely there should be at least a little moisture.

"Nope," Eric said. "No water."

"Thank you for letting me know," she said. "But we may have to dig quite a way to reach water."

"Let me know how it comes out." Eric started to walk away.

"Don't you go anywhere," Daley said.

She jabbed the shovel in again. The sandy soil was hard to dig in. She dug a little deeper, pulled out the dirt, looked in again. Still nothing.

It took her five minutes to enlarge the top of the hole, getting through all the roots and grass. And no sign of water.

Then she started digging deeper. Her shoulders were getting tired, but she kept digging. The soil was heavy and seemed moist. But no water was collecting in the bottom. This was going to be a lot more work than she thought. It killed her to think that she might go to all this trouble and then have nothing to show for it.

Eric sat down on a fallen log nearby—after checking it carefully for leeches. He sat there looking at her while she dug, his chin on his fist. She had enlarged the hole so that it was above her knees—and still no real sign of water. Maybe she'd gotten this all wrong. Maybe it was a waste of time. After a while she looked up and snapped, "Am I boring you?"

"You should probably use your legs more," Eric said. "You're doing it all with your arms. You'll wear yourself out."

She climbed out of the hole, threw the shovel at him. "Show me how it's done," she said.

"I'm speaking strictly from a theoretical perspective," he said.

She stuck the shovel in his face. "Dig."

He stood, stretched, touched his toes, made a big show of getting ready, and then finally took the shovel.

He climbed into the hole, jammed the shovel down, threw a heaping shovelful of soil over his shoulder. Then he stopped, leaned over, and stared intently at the ground.

"Looking won't do it," Daley said. "You have to dig."

But Eric just crooked his finger at her and said, "Look."

She came over and looked into the hole.

"What?" she said.

"Right there." He pointed. And there it was! A tiny trickle of water was coming from one side of the hole. Then water was welling up from the bottom of the hole. Within seconds, the entire bottom of the hole was nearly full of water.

Daley felt her eyes widen. She looked at Eric. He seemed as stunned as she was.

"I did it!" Eric said, waving the shovel triumphantly in the air. Eric climbed out of the hole. His shoes were now sopping wet.

"There must be an underground spring!" she said. "Look! That's got to be at least a gallon of water already."

"Is it drinkable?" Eric said.

"It should be. Taste it."

Eric bent over, then stopped, eyeing the water distrustfully. "No. You taste it."

"I dug. You taste."

Eric blinked. "What do you think I was just doing?"

Daley sighed, then leaned over and scooped up a handful of water. It was a little dirty-looking. Her heart was beating hard suddenly. What if it was poisonous or something? She took a deep breath. Lifted the water to her mouth, touched it with her tongue.

Eric leaned closer in anticipation.

"Tastes okay." She sucked the rest of the water into her mouth. Oh, man! It was a little gritty—but water had never tasted that good to her in her whole life. She hadn't realized just how thirsty she was until just that minute.

Eric's eyes were glued to her face. "Well?"

She smiled.

"What can I say?" Eric said. "My idea worked. I'm a genius."

Back at the beach, Nathan pulled up the side of the tarp, climbed down into the funnel-shaped pit he'd dug. Taylor stood above him, looking down with a bemused expression on her face. He bent over to look into the cup.

"Any water?" Taylor said.

"I can't see," Nathan said. The cup was down in the darkest part of the hole. It just looked like a black circle. He couldn't tell if there was anything in it. Then he saw a gleam of blue light—a reflection of the sky. "Yes!" he said.

He pulled the cup out of the sand, hoisted it into the air. The small clear cup had about an inch and a half of slightly cloudy water in it.

"Check it out!" he said. "It worked. I am psyched!"

Taylor squinted like she was having trouble seeing.

"After only a couple of hours," Nathan said. "Imagine how much we'll have after a whole day!"

Taylor seemed unimpressed. "Maybe about enough for a gerbil?"

"Make fun," Nathan said. "But I have a feeling we are about to get all the water we need."

"Incoming!" a voice yelled.

Nathan whirled around just in time to see Eric running toward him across the sand, waving something at him.

"What the—"

Nathan caught a face full of water. Taylor screamed and jumped out of the way as Eric began squirting water all around them. Daley was behind him. She had an armload of water bottles in her hands.

"We got water!" Daley yelled.

"Loads of it!" Eric said, squirting Nathan in the chest. "More than we need!"

"There's an underground spring in the jungle," Daley added.

Nathan felt a wave of disappointment. Suddenly his little ounce or two of water looked pretty pathetic.

"You mean I can wash my hair?" Taylor said.

"You can wash the whole airplane!" Daley said.

Taylor grabbed a bottle from Eric. Daley squirted her. Taylor squirted back. Nathan's shoulders sagged. Daley and Eric's discovery had pretty much made all his hard work amount to squat.

For a moment he watched the others laughing and squirting one another. Then he thought, *Hey, what's the big deal? We've got water, right? Who cares who found it?*

He looked around. Nobody was watching him at all. He let his little cup of water drain into the sand, then tossed the cup back in the hole. Then he grabbed a bottle of water, aimed it at Daley, and nailed her right in the face.

Daley nailed him right back.

As the water dripped from their faces, their eyes met for a moment. Then they both started laughing.

For the first time since the engines caught fire, Nathan began to feel like maybe things were going to work out okay.

Lex poked his head out of the airplane to see what the noise was all about. Apparently he was still in there working on his mysterious electronic project. Daley turned away from Nathan, squirted Lex.

Funny, Nathan thought. *The last time everything seemed this good was back on the plane when Eric was squirting everybody, pretending he was throwing up on them.*

While the other kids were laughing and squirting one another, Nathan turned and looked out at the water. The sea was a gorgeous blue, the waves rolling in with a calm, steady rhythm.

It's funny how your mood can change, he reflected. Worst-case scenario, now that they had water, they'd be able to hold out for at least a couple of weeks. Even without finding more food. And a lot could happen in a week. Maybe the reason Captain Russell was taking so long was that he'd seen signs of people over on the far side of the island. Maybe he'd had to hike a mile or two farther to find the inhabitants of the island, and now they were on their way back.

Nathan felt a sudden flood of enthusiasm. Everything was going to be fine, right?

Suddenly he was conscious that behind him, everyone had gone silent.

He turned and saw everybody standing there like statues, staring at the jungle. His eyes were adjusting from looking at the bright water and so he couldn't really make out what they were staring at.

There at the edge of the beach, something moved in the jungle.

"Captain Russell?" Melissa said.

TWENTY-TWO

What Daley saw made her heart sink.

It was Captain Russell, alright—Captain Russell and the three kids who'd gone with him. But the grim expression on the pilot's face made it pretty clear that he hadn't found anybody out there.

"So where've you been?"

"What happened?"

"What took you so long?"

There was a chorus of questions. But the pilot didn't answer them.

Captain Russell's face was haggard and sunburned, and he had two days' growth of beard.

"Water," was all he said.

He hobbled slowly across the hot sand, hand extended, wincing with every step.

Daley held out a bottle of the water they'd just gotten from the well she and Eric had made. Lex came out of the plane with a bunch of wires in his hand. His face fell as soon as he saw the weary-looking group.

Captain Russell poured the water into his mouth. Behind him, Jory Twist, Ian Milbauer, and Abby Fujimoto had their hands out, too. Daley helped distribute water to all of them. They, too, sucked it down like they hadn't had anything to drink all day. Which—come to think of it—they probably hadn't.

"Okay," Captain Russell said, looking at the bottle of slightly cloudy water, "that is about the tastiest water I've had in my life. Where'd you get it?"

"Daley and I dug a well," Eric said.

Russell clapped his hand on Eric's shoulder. "Good work."

Eric shrugged modestly. "Hey, I'm just doing what I can."

There was a brief pause.

"So," Nathan said finally, "what happened?"

Captain Russell walked over by the plane, sat down on a piece of driftwood, and pulled off his pink flip-flops—which by now were ragged ruins. His feet didn't look much better. Even with all the dirt that covered them, they were obviously scratched and blistered.

"This island's bigger than I thought," Captain Russell said.

"Yeah," Nathan said. "I went up on the dune over there right after you left and I was looking out—"

Captain Russell looked irritated. "You want to hear my story or not?"

"Sorry," Nathan said.

"So once we got out there, it was obvious the island was bigger than I expected. But beyond that, it's just slow going. Every tree out there is covered with vines and there are ravines that are too steep to climb into and . . . well, bottom line, it wasn't like hiking the Appalachian Trail. I'd say we probably didn't make more than a mile or two the first day. By the time we realized how long it was taking to get anywhere, we determined that we wouldn't make it back by sundown."

Ian spoke up. "What he's saying is we got lost."

Everybody laughed, except Captain Russell. "Hey, we had a compass," he said defensively. "We knew generally which way we were going. But the specifics . . ." He shrugged. "Anyway, next thing we know, it's getting dark. Fortunately Abby had a tarp in her backpack. Good thinking, Abby."

Abby beamed.

"So we got under the tarp, kind of huddled up and tried to sleep. Next thing we know, we're in the middle of a monsoon."

"It was terrible," Jory wailed. "I thought we were gonna die."

"It was a little, uh, exciting for a while," Captain Russell said. "But finally it quit and the sun came up. Basically we spent the rest of the day reconnoitering." He spread his hands. "And here we are."

"So . . . I take it you didn't find signs of anybody out there?" Daley said.

Russell's face darkened a little. "Not yet, no."

Daley frowned. "What do you mean, *not yet?*"

"Oh," Russell said lightly, "we're not staying. We're just coming back for provisions."

"But you *have to* stay," Melissa said. "We need somebody to help us—"

"Decision's made, sweetheart," Russell said.

"We need somebody to take care of us."

"Hey, that's not my strong suit anyway," the pilot said. "But feel free to come with us if you want."

"Come with you where?" Melissa said.

"We found a little ridge about half a mile from here, gave us a pretty good view of the island." He picked up a stick, started drawing a crab-shaped figure in the sand. "We're here on the south end of the island. Reef's here. Big volcanic mountain is over here on the far end of the island. What do you think, kids? Five miles away?"

"Might even be ten," Ian said.

"Whatever," Captain Russell said. "Now obviously we can't see anything from here because of the mountain. But see these here?" He pointed to the drawing of the island in the sand. "These crab-claw shapes? The way they hook around, it looks like there's a natural bay over there on the north side of the island. If anybody lives on this island, they're likely to be fishermen. They'll want to keep their boats in that bay, safe from storms."

"What are you saying?" Daley said.

"We're just here to get provisioned up, then we're heading for the north side of the island."

"Who is?"

Captain Russell stood up, clapped his hands together, pointed at the tub full of dried food. "Ian, grab a couple days' worth of dried food. Abby, you get some water. As much as we can carry."

Ian stood and walked toward the food bin.

"Wait a minute!" Daley said. "That's our food!"

"You can't take all our food!" Nathan said.

Ian reached into the tub, pulled out four more packages, tossed one each to Captain Russell, Jory, and Abby. Then he bit the top off the package in his hand, spit it on the sand.

"We have a rationing plan," Daley said.

But Ian started putting dried food into his backpack.

Daley and Nathan looked at each other.

"Don't take all our food!" Nathan said.

"Yeah," Daley said. "We've only got two days' worth left."

Ian looked uncertainly at Captain Russell. Russell waved his hand in a circle indicating that he should keep going.

"Well, I mean, you've got more, don't you?" Abby said.

Daley ran over and looked in the tub. There was hardly any food left. Maybe ten packages. With seven kids to feed, that was one meal. Two if they stretched it. Ian was buckling up his daypack.

"This is it," Daley said. "There's no more."

"Dude!" Eric said. "This isn't fair!"

"You haven't left us with *anything*," Daley said.

"Hey, if we find people over there, it won't matter how much food you've got," Captain Russell said.

"And if you don't?"

Russell waved his hands at the jungle. "We just walked through a grove full of coconuts. All you gotta do is go out there and throw a rock into a tree and you'll have plenty to eat. You guys have all day to sit around figuring out ways to find more. Not us. We'll be traveling and we won't be able to goof around looking for food."

"*Goof* around?" Nathan said. "Why don't *you* try getting those coconuts out of the tree?"

"You guys are doing great here." The pilot gave Nathan a thin, somewhat insincere smile and gestured at the camp. "Look, you pitched tents, you found water . . . I have every confidence in you."

Nathan and Daley exchanged glances.

"Do something!" Nathan said.

"*You* do something," Daley said.

"This totally isn't fair," Nathan said.

Captain Russell looked around the group and said, "And

if we drop dead of starvation ten feet before we reach help? Huh? Does that work for you?"

Everyone was silent.

A container of food fell out of Ian's backpack, spilled onto the ground. Jory scooped it up and put it back into Ian's backpack.

Suddenly Jackson stepped forward. "Put some back," he said softly.

Ian looked at him nervously.

Jackson reached out with the sharp stick he carried, tapped Ian's backpack, then pointed at the tub.

"Uh . . ." Ian said. He looked over at Captain Russell again.

Captain Russell's jaw clamped shut. "Hey, kid, we need the food."

Jackson glanced at him momentarily, then looked back at Ian. He tapped the tub again with his spear. "Put. It. Back."

"Are you threatening somebody?" Captain Russell said. Jackson ignored him.

Ian looked at the pilot, then at Jackson, then at the pilot. Finally he fumbled with the pack and started pulling out the packages of dried food, tossing them into the bin.

"Who died and made you king?" Captain Russell said. "We need that food."

Ian kept putting packages back into the bin. Finally Jackson said, "Stop."

Captain Russell wiped the top of his balding head.

Jackson turned to the pilot. "Four of you, seven of us. You're getting half the food. That's more than fair."

Captain Russell scowled. But he didn't say anything. Finally he looked around and said, "I need better shoes. Anybody got a spare pair of shoes?"

Spare shoes? Daley couldn't believe the guy had flown halfway across the Pacific in a pair of flip-flops—and hadn't even brought a spare pair of shoes.

"Maybe I could wrap towels around my feet or something," the pilot mumbled, seemingly to himself.

"Wait a second," Lex said. "While I was working in the plane, I saw something." He went back in the plane, still carrying a bunch of wires in his hand. When he came back, he had left the wires in the plane and was carrying a pair of extremely old, extremely large, extremely worn white canvas tennis shoes. "I found them behind the pilot's seat."

Captain Russell looked at them dubiously. They were obviously too big for him. "Well, it's something," he said.

Everyone stood around glumly as he rifled through boxes until finally he came across a towel. He tore strips off the towel and stuffed them into the toes of the shoes. When he was done, he put his feet in them. There was a ripping sound and a hole appeared in the top of one of them. His big toe poked out through the ancient canvas.

"You sure you don't want to stay the night?" Melissa said. "It might be nice if . . ."

Russell looked up at her and something in his eyes made her voice trail off. It took a moment for Daley to figure out what she saw in his face. But then she realized. Fear. Captain Russell was very afraid.

No one had quite said it out loud, but they'd been pinning all their hopes on him. Captain Russell was going to figure things out. Captain Russell was going to fix their problems. Captain Russell was going to find help.

It settled over her like a dark cloud. If Captain Russell was just as afraid as they were, then . . .

Then what?

Then, they were in trouble. They were really, truly in trouble.

"Captain Russell?" Nathan said. "Are you sure you want to do this? I mean, if you get out there and your feet get all cut up and infected and stuff. Or . . . I mean . . . what if you get lost again?"

Russell looked up at him angrily. "You got a better idea? The radio's useless, there're no search planes flying over, no pleasure cruisers sailing by, no nothing. I'm not just gonna sit here praying while the food runs out. I'm not!"

Nathan looked away.

"Let him go," Daley said. "Either he'll find help or he won't."

"We already had this argument once," Nathan said. "Let's not do it again."

"For once I agree with you," Daley said.

Captain Russell stood up, looked down at his huge, tattered shoes. If it hadn't been such a bad situation, they would have looked comical.

"So that's it then," he said. "We're gonna go. Try and make a little headway before the sun goes down."

"I've got water," Abby said.

"Everybody saddle up," Captain Russell said. "Put as much water in your packs as you can carry."

Abby, Ian, and Jory finished loading the water, then began following Captain Russell toward the jungle. They all looked bone tired.

Just as they were about to reach the trees, a voice called out, "Hey!"

It was Jackson.

Captain Russell turned. When he saw that Jackson was walking toward him, he said, "You again?"

Jackson stopped, pulled off his sneakers, held them out to Captain Russell.

Captain Russell frowned in puzzlement for a moment, then reached out and took the shoes.

"Here," Jackson said, thrusting his pointed stick into the ground next to Captain Russell. "You might need it."

Then he turned and walked barefoot back toward the plane.

Captain Russell picked up the shoes, looked inside them. "Size eleven," he said. "Hey, that's my size."

TWENTY-THREE

Later that evening everyone was sitting around the fire. The sun had just slipped over the horizon leaving a fiery blaze of red on the western sky. The night didn't seem quite so frightening as it had. *It's strange,* Nathan thought. *To look at us, you'd think we're just a bunch of ordinary kids hanging out at the beach after a Friday night football game.*

"Look!" Nathan said. "First star."

There, gleaming above them in the darkening sky, was a brilliant white point of light.

"First star I see tonight, I wish I may, I wish I might, have the wish I wish tonight," Melissa said.

"What are you wishing for?" Taylor said.

"Duh," Daley said.

Taylor looked around the circle. "What?"

Everybody laughed except Taylor.

"More water anyone?" Daley said.

"Right here," Taylor said. Daley handed her a full bottle

of water. Taylor squeezed it into her mouth. "Eeeeyew! It's hot."

"We had to boil it," Melissa said. "To make sure it's safe."

"Plus we couldn't find an ice machine," Eric said.

Nathan held up his water bottle. "A toast. Here's to Captain Russell. I hope he finds somebody out there."

Everyone lifted the bottles.

"Also, uh . . . I hate to admit it, but here's to Daley and Eric. There's no other way to put this. They saved our lives."

Everybody cheered and raised their water bottles. Nathan tipped his bottle toward Daley. She clicked her bottle against his. Water sloshed onto the sand. It was a relief not to have to worry about that. It felt good not to be at each other's throats.

"We never found out who stole the water," Lex said.

Nathan noticed Daley and Eric sharing a look.

"What?" Nathan said to Daley.

"Uh . . ." Daley looked momentarily uncomfortable. "That's my bad."

She opened the lid of the cooler. It was full of water bottles. "False alarm. I found them. I'd stuck them somewhere when I was getting everything organized. Totally forgot. Sorry for making everyone nuts."

"That's okay, Daley," Eric said. "Everyone makes mistakes."

Nathan studied Eric's face. He always looked like he was making some kind of joke, so it was hard to know when he was being serious and when he was jerking you around. Before Nathan could come to any sort of conclusion about what was passing between Daley and Eric, Jackson stood up.

"I got something to say," Jackson said.

Everybody looked at one another. It was the first time

Jackson had made any sort of attempt to say anything to the whole group—aside from when he was stopping other people from fighting.

"Look, I'm kind of an every-man-for-himself guy," Jackson said. "But I've been thinking. That's probably a stupid way of doing things here. We need to pull together. If we're not a team, we're not gonna make it."

"Yeah," Nathan said.

"So . . ." Jackson looked around the group. The faces of all the kids flickered in the firelight. Behind him the red light of the sky had faded to a dark purple. His face was half shadowed now, eyes invisible. "So, if you guys still want me, I want to give a shot at being the leader."

Nathan wasn't sure how he felt. He looked over at Daley to see her reaction. She was looking at him—obviously wanting to know the same thing. The truth was, this rivalry between them was not doing anybody any good. Maybe it was best this way. Nathan looked around to see how the others were reacting.

Melissa's face had broken into a broad grin. Boy, this obviously made her day! She was looking raptly at Jackson, her black eyes shining in the firelight. Nathan felt a brief stab of jealousy. But then it passed.

"Okay, chief," Eric drawled. "How's this gonna work?"

"I think we should all do what we're good at."

There was silence for a moment, then everyone nodded their heads.

"Daley?" Jackson said.

"Why don't I keep dealing with food and water? I'll handle keeping the well maintained, boiling the water, rationing food, scheduling the meals . . ."

"Good," Jackson said. "Nathan?"

"Well," Nathan said. "I think I want to keep working on finding food. I know it's out there. There's fish, fruit, shellfish, coconuts ... With a little help, I'm sure I can get us a more reliable food supply. Plus I can work on finding other stuff in the jungle that will come in handy. Building materials, wood we could use to make boats or bows and arrows with, rocks we could use to make arrowheads with ..."

"Great," Jackson said. "What about you, Melissa?"

"What if I'm responsible for the fire? I gather firewood, tend the fire, make sure that we're storing enough wood. Also I can help out with the cooking. Maybe Daley and I could do that together."

Jackson nodded. "Taylor?"

Taylor blinked. "Uh." She looked around furtively. Her eyes landed on the video camera. "I know! We need batteries for a lot of important things. The lights, the camera, anything else that Lex gets working. I'll make sure they're all charged up so we can use them whenever we need them."

"Good," Jackson said. "That leaves you, Eric."

"Moi?" Eric looked around the circle. Nobody spoke. Finally he said, "You know, it really sounds like you guys have everything covered. I was thinking I'd just kinda backstop the rest of you. Like, I'd just sort of reserve my strength and fill in if anybody gets sick or whatever."

Jackson looked at him, most of his face still shrouded in darkness.

"You're giving me that scary look, Jackson." Eric had his Mr. Innocence face on. "Go ahead, make your point. I'm sure you have one."

"Somebody needs to haul water back from the well."

Eric's eyebrows shot up. "Oh, no! Not me. I got this tendinitis thing, see." He rubbed his right elbow and winced. "My doctor gave me very strict instructions not use my right hand. He said I might lose the arm."

Jackson went over to the plane, came back with a large canteen, tossed it to Eric. "So use your left arm."

Everyone laughed. Eric caught the canteen, then held it out at arm's length like it might bite him. "What about Junior?" he said finally. "Doesn't Lex get a job?"

"His job is to think of ways to help us get by."

"No, no, see that's the thing," Eric said. "That's *exactly* what I'm good at. Thinking!"

"Hey, yeah," Taylor said, "that's no fair that Lex gets to lounge around while I'm working my fingers to the bone."

Jackson held up his hands. Everyone quieted down suddenly. "The little guy has been busy." He looked over at Lex and nodded.

Lex said, "We don't know how long we're gonna be here. I guess the only thing we know for sure is that we all want to go home. I figured as long as we were stuck, we might as well try to make it feel as much like home as we can."

He walked over to the plane, picked up an mp3 player that was sitting on one of the camp chairs near the hatch. A pair of wires trailed from the mp3 player into the plane. Nathan wondered what the kid was up to.

"Daley said she missed music," Lex said. "So . . ."

He pressed the PLAY button on the mp3 player.

Suddenly music poured out of a pair of speakers that Lex had set up on the top of the plane. It wasn't loud, but still—it sounded great. It was a song that had been playing on the radio all the time before they'd left.

Before they'd left. The words had a strange ring to them. It had only been a couple of days . . . but it seemed like it had been forever.

Nathan grinned.

After a minute Taylor got up and started to dance. Then she crooked her finger at Eric. Eric just about broke his legs jumping up to dance with her. Melissa started dancing, then Daley got up, pulled Lex to his feet, and joined in.

For a minute Nathan just lay there. The beach spread

itself out in front of him, the water beyond it slightly phosphorescent. Up in the sky the bright star he'd spotted was surrounded by other stars now, all of them impossibly bright. Back in LA you'd never see this many stars—not even in the middle of the night.

He fixed his eye on the brightest star and thought, *Okay, it's just a silly superstition—but why not?*

Star light, star bright. First star I see tonight, I wish I may, I wish I might, have the wish I wish tonight.

And then the wish itself: *Please get us home. Please, please, please.*

Melissa reached over and grabbed his hand, hoisted him to his feet. He wasn't that big on dancing. It made him feel stupid, like everybody was looking at him. But something about the moment made him feel free and not self-conscious. He began to move.

They all danced, everyone grinning and laughing like this was the greatest thing that had ever happened in their lives. All of them except Jackson, that is.

Nathan noticed that Jackson stood away from the group, arms folded, face lost in the darkness. He looked haunted and vaguely dangerous. Like some ancient soldier preparing for battle.

What was it that Nathan's great-great-grandfather had written in his book? *The leader is always the loneliest of men.*

For a moment Nathan felt relieved—relieved not to be the guy who worried about shelter and water and food and latrines and who was getting along and who wasn't. He closed his eyes and let the music sink into his bones.

Let tomorrow take care of itself. Tomorrow.